WILD ROSE COUNTRY

X·14·11

Stories from Alberta

Stories by Rudy Wiebe,
Edward McCourt,
Georges Bugnet, Earle Birney,
Betty Wilson, Helen Rosta,
Robert Kroetsch,
W. O. Mitchell,
Stephen Scobie, Henry Kreisel,
Dorothy Livesay,
George Bowering
and Margaret Atwood.

Edited by David Carpenter

Introduction

This book is a collection of thirteen stories by writers who were born and raised in Alberta or who lived there long enough to write about it. They are not merely regional stories; their appeal is in no way restricted. Yet they belong to their region in many of their individual details. And collectively they are an expression of Alberta's regional psychology. Perhaps mythology is a better word. For it is a region's myths, embedded in narratives such as these, that map out the distinctive contours of a region's psyche.

When I think of the Alberta psyche I think of a vast procession of promoters: snake-oil salesmen, whisky traders, gold prospectors, Bible-thumping preachers, government land agents, radio station disc jockeys, jowly rotarians, messianic politicians, smiling tourist-information girls, natty public relations officers and paunchy oil executives. And since well before 1905, when Alberta became a province, they have been eulogizing her virtues in a way that makes her the ego capital of Canada. I say "her" for special reasons. Alberta was named, by men of course, after the fourth daughter of Queen Victoria. And the promoters I speak of have often retained the feminine analogy, especially to describe the land itself. Here is a recent and very typical eulogy: "Alberta is a sober young lady who methodically plans for her future. She is also beautiful, unpredictable. . . and rich. How can I help but be in love with her?" (Walter Petrigo, *Petrigo's Alberta*). Soldiers of fortune for two centuries have travelled to Alberta, beheld her many-faceted charms, imposed their dreams of paradise upon her rose-scattered beauty and sold her bounty for a sizeable profit to men as romantic or as zealous as they. The first of these amorous white conquerors of the late eighteenth century, such as Anthony Henday and Peter Pond, came with rifles. Now they come with oil drills. It begins with love. It ends with exploitation. The virgin land of wild roses, a new version of mother earth, the "sober young lady," is sent out into the street to sell her wares. And Alberta's mythology, present in the best of her fiction from Arthur Stringer's *Prairie Wife* (1915) to Robert Kroetsch's *Badlands* (1976), is haunted by strains of romantic promise and romantic disenchantment.

Let us ask the inevitable question: what is it about the provincial kingdom of Alberta that gives these stories a distinctive flavour? What in Alberta's history, for example, separates it so firmly from Saskatchewan, with which it shares a 750-mile border? To an Albertan during or since the Depression, any tendency to lump the two provinces together is a little like lumping together Egypt and the Promised Land at the time of the Seven Plagues.

Alberta is a special sort of Promised Land, however. It is not the Promised Land for the already-successful, for the genteel, for the retired company man, for the soporific and serene. Everyone knows that's British Columbia: that pasture beyond the mountains, that oasis of retirement (and sometimes even socialism), that last misty stopover preparatory to the Final Voyage West. Rather, Alberta is a Promised Land for the young at heart and vigorous of body: the bone-hard rancher of the southern short-grass plains, the sturdy Ukrainian wheat farmer, the self-made man who believes in the power of positive thinking and the lore of the fast buck. So if ever that fading American Dream of romantic individualism evaporates in arid cynicism, one can be fairly certain that there will still be a solid contingent of Alberta promoters singing out for frontier conservatism. And more recently there are among them the zealots who cry out for separatism.

The Alberta psyche can be discussed in historical-political terms just as relevantly as in geographic, economic or literary terms. In electing two non-aligned parties, the United Farmers of Alberta (1921 to 1935) and the Social Credit Party (1935 to 1971), the people of Alberta both revealed and nurtured their unique political character. And of course Alberta's regional distinction is directly related to its geography. I do not mean simply Alberta's tourist geography—its Rockies and foothills. I mean too its unusually rich oil and mining resources. These aesthetic and monetary riches have shaped the emergence of Alberta's mythology, one which has its beginnings at least 30 years before Alberta became a province in 1905.

There was relative peace and order, after the arrival of the Mounted Police in the area that is now Southern Alberta, from 1874 to 1885. And even during the rebellion year, the fighting was largely suppressed within Alberta: it was confined to the area east of Frog Lake. The arrival of the railroad in Calgary in 1883 and the passing of the buffalo from the plains (approximately 1881 to 1884) coincided with Sitting Bull's retreat to the United States.

Years of relative prosperity followed those early years of peace. Coal mining in the province had been gathering momentum since 1870. The ranching industry received a shot in the arm from the unusual demand for beef in the Klondike during the closing years of the century. Serious oil exploration and drilling began in 1914. These relatively pleasant conditions were a prelude to the unusually fortunate events that followed decades later. In the great depression of the thirties, Alberta was the prairie province least injured by drought. Its drought was the financial one that brought forth such maverick economic solutions and theories. By contrast, Saskatchewan was ravaged by physical drought during those years.

7

Not that Albertans had an easy time of it during the Depression. They did not, but their recovery in the forties was unlike that of any province in the country. After the oil boom in 1947 and the subsequent influx of American capital and settlement, an industrial, mining, and general population boom, Alberta boasted that it was the richest per capita province in Canada. In spite of formidable municipal debts within the province, Alberta has claimed, until recently, to be the only debt-free province in the country. Nowhere else in Canada is the lure of quick fortune felt as it is in Alberta.

This tradition too is related to Alberta's maverick political history. Albertans have a reputation for being suspicious of eastern interests. They proved it with their creation of the UFA party; they proved it again with their creation of the Social Credit party which, according to Aberhart, was a force to combat the "Eastern Conspiracy." Of course it cannot be denied that all western provinces have shown a suspicion of eastern political motives. But Alberta was the last western province to be settled, and among the prairie provinces, the most remote from Ontario. It is not difficult to see a sense of antipathy toward federal political concerns proportionate to Alberta's geographical distance from the power centres of the East.

Alberta's unique political allegiances appear to have crystallized between the time of the rise of the UFA party and Aberhart's landslide victory of 1935. A wave of populist sympathies had been sweeping Canada from a few years before the turn of the century to the early nineteen-twenties. These sympathies were largely promoted by Protestant churchmen and rooted in Protestant ethics, but they led to collectivist organizations. One such organization, which had more than a taste of methodism in it, was Saskatchewan's CCF party. The collectivist spirit and its political manifestations in Saskatchewan were largely the dirt farmers' response to the physical and financial drought of the thirties.

But in Alberta conditions were different. First, the province

8

was settled by a large proportion of people who belonged to (or joined) evangelical sects and cults; in Saskatchewan the nationally aligned churches, established Protestant denominations, seemed to dominate. Secondly, while the financial drought was general across the province, the physical drought was totally destructive only in the southeast corner and scattered areas north of there. Thirdly, while the Depression raged in scattered parts of Alberta, the people's regional heritage militated strongly against anything that smacked of socialism. This heritage was kept alive by the large number of expectant capitalists who had in various ways created Alberta's Promised Land mythology: the thousands of unsuccessful Klondikers who settled in and around Edmonton, and their progeny; the thousands of Southern Alberta ranchers whose lifestyle was the embodiment of independence and romantic individualism; the dirt farmers who, in so many cases, were able to harvest a crop during the drought years.

Was this Promised Land mythology and its political consequences a fundamentalist reaction to the social gospel? Or was this mytho-political phenomenon simply the expectant capitalists' reaction to creeping socialism? In either case, the focus for Alberta's economic and religious eccentricities was eventually William Aberhart. He was the radio Messiah to the weary and heavy laden. He was the enemy of the usurer but the friend of the independent commodity producer like R. J. C. Stead's fictional hero of *Dennison Grant* (1920).

It is not difficult to demonstrate Alberta's political individuality and the social forces behind its political masks. Nowhere in Canada had two consecutive non-aligned parties been able to seize power in a province as the UFA and the Social Credit party had done in 1921 and 1935. Nowhere in Canada had such vacillations between left and right been seen in so short a time. Both the UFA and the Social Credit parties had begun as radical populist alternatives to the federally represented parties. Both, by the end of their tenure, were ultra conserva-

9

tive governments.

Albertans had scarcely any radical tradition: socialist, revolutionary or whatever; no Louis Riel as Manitobans had and a relatively weak tradition of collectivism unlike that of, say, the Saskatchewan farmers. In 1943, when Manning took over the premiership, his election victories were founded on the fight against socialism as much as on the fight for Social Credit. The present government in Alberta is Conservative. It is neither presumptive nor clairvoyant to say that no province in the country is more securely in the hands of Conservatives (be they Joe Clark's or Peter Lougheed's), which is to say, in Alberta, safer from the seductions of socialism. It is true that in the elections of 1921 and 1935 one witnessed the banding together of the oppressed little man against the money interests of the "Eastern Conspiracy." It is true as well that in Alberta's unique system of delegate democracy (under Aberhart) one witnessed a radical espousal of the one-party system. And it is true that both the UFA and the Social Credit governments maintained that they were run directly by the mass desire of the people.

But Fortune has endowed Alberta with enough prosperity to allow it to perpetuate a romantic vision seen, as it were, through wild-rose-coloured glasses. To the fundamentalist it announces itself in the imagery of the Promised Land. To the expectant capitalist it seeks expression in treasure-hunt narratives. To the tourist or outdoorsman it finds its romantic backdrop in the northern forests or the Rockies. It should be noted that the bases for three romantic myths are suggested here, and that these myths are far from compatible. Such are the historical paradoxes of a province whose economy and social structure have been accelerated at an unusually rapid rate from a pastoral to an urbanized condition.

Saskatchewan's embracing of collectivism and socialism and rejection of Social Credit during the thirties was consistent with its regionally dictated survival mythology. And Alberta's embracing of Social Credit (thanks to the optimistic monetary reformers' theorizing) and rejection of socialism was consistent with its regionally dictated Promised Land mythology.

The late Edward McCourt, in his travel book *Saskatchewan,* puts it this way: "The Saskatchewan man has thus been shaped by a sterner physical environment than that of most Canadians. Having been compelled to adapt himself to that environment, he has made his own rules for survival and looks with suspicion on traditional values cherished in softer lands. He tends to take a less optimistic view of life than do his neighbours, particularly those who live in Alberta."

In most of Saskatchewan's serious fiction, hanging on against great odds is the key theme; "making it" is out of the question. In McCourt's *Music at the Close,* an Alberta novel, his protagonist is always seeking the pot of gold at the end of the rainbow. In his *Home is the Stranger,* a typical Saskatchewan novel, his protagonist is severely demoralized because of the total absence of rainbows to chase (let alone pots of gold).

W. O. Mitchell's settings are divided evenly between Saskatchewan and Alberta. His *Jake and the Kid* stories and *Who Has Seen the Wind* are set in Saskatchewan. The severities of farm life during the Depression and World War 2 are recounted with warmth, humour and acceptance, affecting people unable to do much more than learn to live with them. In *The Kite* and *The Vanishing Point,* set in Alberta, the protagonists (David Lang and Carlyle Sinclair) are questers of a romantic cast. They seek and find love and serenity in a pristine setting. They discover in Alberta what Ralph Allen's heroine is seeking in *Peace River Country* by fleeing Saskatchewan for Alberta.

Sinclair Ross declares himself a Saskatchewan writer. While writing his classic *As For Me and My House* he undoubtedly remembered Stringer's sentimental Alberta *Prairie Trilogy* (1922) and managed to avoid its romantic excesses. The plots

11

of the two works are remarkably similar in that they are both narrated from the point of view of a prairie woman who is progressively more estranged from her husband's love as the story proceeds. Both women are classical pianists who seek the friendship of local school teachers who, in both cases, are pedantic philologists. The parallels can be extended, but the differences are, again from a regional point of view, very significant. Chaddie McKail, the Alberta protagonist, prospers in love, divorce and alimony; but Mrs. Bentley, the Saskatchewan protagonist, hangs on grimly to her broken, brooding man.

I mentioned that the emergent Alberta myth seems to have something to do with turning the rose-strewn wilderness into a prosperous Promised Land. It is amusing to see this belief expressed in the popular literature of the oil-boom days. Here are two examples from *Chinook Arch* (1967), a collection of miscellaneous pieces by local Alberta writers.

> . . . today I saw a buck deer watch with *placid, unconcerned* liquid eyes, as an oil derrick was being erected nearby. He stood in the edge of a thicket, his colours blending perfectly with the foliage—as still as a statue. A red squirrel scurried up the trunk of a tree. Two crows scolded furiously, for I had penetrated too close to their sacred domain. A porcupine waddled *unconcernedly* down the path. The old pulsating beat of life was all about me. I felt proud—and awed —and with the greater wisdom that had been its gift to me, I echoed Mike's words: "I am an Albertan."

> The oil boom, bigger now than even the prophets dreamed, *planted the derricks that blossom* against the skyline.

Both of these quotations, by different authors, are naïve expressions of the Alberta popular imagination which aspires in countless fictions to the illusion of an unmolested, natural Eden blossoming with roses and forests and oil derricks, festooned with bull market ticker tape. This is surely one of the basic paradoxes of the Alberta character.

It was this unheard-of wealth that kept the Manning administration, which began just before the great oil strike at Leduc and ended with Manning's retirement at the peak of Alberta prosperity in 1968, in power so long. It could maintain its politically unique status, achieved during the thirties, because it could afford such eccentric tastes. In a sense, Alberta's bumper crops, its cattle, its coal and other minerals, and especially its oil and gas, were the fulfillment of the Moses-like prophesies of Aberhart and Manning. The dream had always been there, or at least since the lure of the Klondike in 1898, which in part put the province of Alberta and the city of Edmonton on the map. Alberta's provincial emblem may be the wild rose, but its flagpole is the oil derrick.

Particularly since the discovery of oil in Alberta, however, the Promised Land myth has become less associated with the unfulfilled aspirations and desperate optimism of Next Year Country and more associated with the guilt-tinged assurances of the Promised Land. And guilt—not tranquillity—seems to accompany the consciousness of a people involved in the invasion of its own wilderness to assure its own prosperity. The two-sided promise, then, of prosperity and wilderness escape, is propelled initially by a romantic dream, but its backlash is a nightmare.

It makes sense, then, that Rory Napoleon, the Métis protagonist of W. O. Mitchell's "Patterns," should want to lash out against the smug patterns of his prosperous little town. He releases a herd of goats into the heart of town on a Saturday night and the result is "Hell [let] out for recess." And in Robert Kroetsch's *The Studhorse Man* and *Gone Indian*, for example, animal stampedes (respectively horses and buffalo) disrupt the artificial patterns of the city of Edmonton. (I will return to this theme in connection with Margaret Atwood's story.)

13

In Robert Kroetsch's story "The Harvester," set in a prairie town, the action is divided between the present world of fast profit, short-order greasy-spoon cafés and flashbacks to the past (a heroic world of epic physical labours); and the compassionate impulses of characters are imprisoned by commercial ones. The story arises quite naturally out of a provincial milieu where sudden wealth and its attendant commercial value structure are impinging upon people whose values were nurtured in a more humane and pastoral setting.

I say "pastoral" because it was a rural environment and one, as Kroetsch must have witnessed it in his boyhood, endowed with the kind of rustic heartiness associated with the days when harvesting was done by men, women and horses. I do not imply that those were easy times, that evil was not present, or that men and women were better. I mean that values were less geared to commercial or corporate success; and avarice, hatred and tragedy wore a different mask. And storytelling takes on different contours to come to terms with this earlier ethic. Wiebe's story of Indian warfare, "Along the Red Deer and the South Saskatchewan," reads like a Homeric epic, a form well suited to articulating the warrior mentality; Bugnet's tale of a superstitious would-be murderer, tortured by guilt, "Mahigan's Atonement," like a primitive version of a biblical allegory. Yet both of these stories are dependent upon an accurate rendering of their Alberta setting. Even the kaleidoscopic orgy of colour in Bugnet's description of the northern lights is accurately reported. It is based on an experience he had watching them one night in November, 1918, at Lac Majeau, which is the story's setting. Regional literature reaches the universal through the particular, and Wiebe and Bugnet demonstrate this in much of their longer fiction as well.

Three other rural stories deserve mention in this connection. They are Earle Birney's Banff story, "Mickey Was a Swell Guy," Betty Wilson's farm story, "White Mountains in the Moon," and particularly Edward McCourt's "The White Mustang." Birney and Wilson both use the Alberta Rockies in a way that has become characteristic of Alberta writers: the backdrop of a story in which there is a poignant sense of loss. It might be the loss of a great friend (Birney's narrative poem, "David"), a beloved (Kroetsch's novella *But We Are Exiles*), a mythic hero (Howard O'Hagan's splendid romance, *Tay John*), or simply one's own equilibrium (Edward McCourt's novel, *Music at the Close*). The examples from Alberta fiction since the thirties are legion. The Rockies, rising as they do so suddenly from the prairie and the foothills, impose not only an end to westward wandering, but perhaps assault the senses with the promise of great heights of romantic aspiration. The pervasive sense of romantic disenchantment seems inevitable.

In Birney's story we are led to a point of view superior to that of the naïve lad who tells the story, and from that point of view we contemplate the death of heroes. In Wilson's story we must piece together the tale of a farming couple's tragic, courageous struggle from the fragments of her confused memory. In both stories there is a painful awareness that certain glories have passed from the earth.

For dreamers who persist in pursuing these old glories, there are certain pitfalls. Perhaps no prairie writer is more aware of the pitfalls awaiting the romantic dreamer than the late Edward McCourt. In his story "The White Mustang," Dermot O'Donnell and his son Jed are two such dreamers. Dermot tells Jed that the horse he has recently seen is a legendary white mustang that has never been corralled. Jed's mother knows the source of Dermot's tale: the Irish myth of Naim the Goldenhaired, the son of Finn. When Jed finds the horse, dead and decaying, he comes down to earth, like the son of Finn in the myth, with a crash. What place have mythic glories in this ambiguous terrain?

The question goes unanswered in the contemporary, urban stories in this collection. But it is addressed in other Alberta fiction by Howard O'Hagan, Henry Kreisel, Edward McCourt and Robert Kroetsch (*Badlands* is an excellent example). The stories from contemporary life in this collection focus on more complex questions. Stephen Scobie, with considerable wit, turns to art; Henry Kreisel directs his ironic sensibility to the question, both horrifying and necessary, of evaluating a moral truth; Dorothy Livesay focuses with much compassion on a generation gap; Helen Rosta looks unflinchingly upon the nature of victimization; George Bowering endorses the elevating nature of actual experience compared with passive spectating. It is the same space but a different time. Now it is the suburbanites and their children who victimize the weaker species, human or otherwise ("Magpie"); the executives who violate the moral codes ("An Anonymous Letter"); the newlyweds who are wanting in compassion ("The Wedding"); the college professor who fights and fornicates his way through the raging emptiness of the foothills ("The Elevator"). Calgary, that is.

Margaret Atwood's bleak and searching story, "Polarities," concludes this collection on a note of controlled but chilling despair. Like so many Alberta narratives which assault the frigidly fixed patterns of a town's complacency, its theme is the need for the integration of a fragmented society. It was written in a series of very close observations of the winters in Edmonton and the terrain immediately east of there. Her protagonist, an American scholar, learns about his limited capacity to love and learns of the dangers of that love. It necessitates a commitment he cannot sustain.

This book of stories has an analogous message for the past, present and future lovers of that lovely wild rose beneath the shadows of the Rockies. It is the message of consciousness, of moral awareness. It reminds Albertans who they were, who they are and who they might be. It tells people everywhere about the passing glories and present frenzies of the Promised Land. And it suggests with perception and compassion the human values that must endure if wild roses are to bloom.

16

For more social background, the reader might like to consult the following: Richard Allen, *The Social Passion*; James MacGregor, *A History of Alberta*; Edward McCourt, *Saskatchewan*; Robert Kroetsch, *Alberta*; John Blackburn, *Land of Promise*; W. E. Mann, *Sect, Cult and Church in Alberta*; James Gray, *The Winter Years*; C. B. Macpherson, *Democracy in Alberta*; J. A. Irving, *The Social Credit Movement in Alberta*; and Jean Burnet, *Next-Year Country*.

Along the Red Deer and South Saskatchewan

To the memory of Little Bear and F. W. Spicer

Rudy Wiebe

This is long ago. Before whites dared to come into our country, when they built the Big House they call Edmonton now and then Little Big House at the edge of our country and barred the doors and put cannons on the corners and let our people through one small door one at a time when we came to trade. We were camped along the Red Deer that winter, for the buffalo would go there under the trees and we followed them. One day that winter Appino-kommit was gone. We didn't think about that, since he never said where he was going, or when. He was a very young man who thought longer than he spoke, and the Old Men sometimes called him crazy head because he had already led boys his own age in a good raid and the older warriors hated him because they were jealous of the coups he brought back. But we, we loved him.

After many days my young brother told me Appino-kommit had come back and wanted to see me at the Antelope Butte. So I went there. His face was burned by the wind and his moccasins worn out; I saw war in his face and I loved him. He told me he had gone three days down the Great River from the forks where the Red Deer joins it and had found a camp of 25 lodges. When he said this he swung his hand flat across his throat, the sign for our enemies the Plains Cree, and I was very happy. He had watched that camp till the sun went down, but then it began to snow and he had to leave because they would see his trail in the snow. He had wanted to watch them one more day, it was foolish for such a small camp to be there alone, but the snow made him come away.

"We start this tonight," he said. "I want 300 young men to meet me at the Lone Tree Crossing when the moon rises. Tell them just that, no more, and they are not to talk to me today because then the chiefs will guess something and tell us not to do it."

I did as he said, and when the moon came up over the Great Lone Tree the young men started coming out of the darkness, all quiet; no-one knew that anyone but himself had been called. But when they saw all the others around them, their faces shone with happiness for they saw there was much to do. Silently we followed Appino-kommit and he led us across the white flats and into the thick trees and willows. There, where we could not be seen, we built small fires and made our quiet prayers to The Great One, asking help, and when that was done everyone told the others of each wrong he had done, both great and small, so that if he didn't come back no man could say, when his deeds were told in the Great Medicine Lodge, that any shame had been hidden in his heart to blacken the glory of his death; that he had faced the enemy with his warcry and his name the last brave sound he would make.

All day we lay under the trees and at night we ran until the line of light grew so wide in our faces that we had to return to the river valley for the day shelter of trees. On the sixth night our run was short. Appino-kommit told us we should sleep till he called us, but I don't know if anyone slept. Just at dawn he came among us and said we should put out the fires.

"Eat all you can," he said. "Who can say who will eat again?"

The snow was almost to our knees and the sun shone on it like fire leaping in the cold. Appino-kommit led us through the brush of the coulee and soon we heard dogs, then horses, and children laughing, and I think I have never heard so many women sing so happily or their axes ring as loud as they did that morning, but I may have forgotten it. But that day I will never forget, and we were not listening for such happy sounds that day, we were very busy. The fire of war burned in us, our enemies were there and we looked at each other and saw war paint. We stripped off our clothes very fast, everything but breechcloths and moccasins lay on the snow, a great pile of clothes, and my young brother had to stay there with them. This made him very sad, but Appino-kommit said it was glory enough for someone so young to be one of a war party as famous as this one would be, so we left him there smiling. I don't know what happened to him; I never saw him again.

We were divided into equal parties, Appino-kommit leading one and Kristo-koom-epoka the other. One party would follow the coulee to where it spread out into the river valley and the edge of the camp, the other would go higher, along the edge of the brush above and then, on a given signal, both would rush into the camp from opposite directions and meet in the centre, as nearly as possible. Women and children wouldn't be touched if they didn't fight. My friend, that was the time to see Appino-kommit; you would have known as we did that he was born to be a warrior. He told every man what to do, nothing was forgotten. "The Crees make it easy for us," he said. "Such a small camp should have scouts out all the time." We looked at each other and then our swift feet carried us apart, but I like to remember that little bit of time, to remember us all together and how I felt the fire of the coming battle jerk my heart for happiness, remember my sad young brother sitting on the pile our clothing made and Appino-kommit, our leader, his war feathers quivering about his proud head in the sunlight so bright and cold, his eyes finding each one of us down to our very hearts as we stood around him. Proud and happy.

The last legging had fallen on the pile and my brother was hardly seated when the word came and we broke into our two parties, running silently, crouched, to the proper place. I was with Kristo-koom-epoka on the left, running with my good friends down the coulee and already I could hear the roar of victory, the brave deeds being sung again in the Medicine Lodge, and I thought of two eyes shining and soft skin flushed soft red as I told what I had done, I a warrior with coups at my belt who needed to fear nothing, certainly not to ask for a girl since everyone knows a warrior needs a wife to keep his lodge. My heart was pounding so hard with these happy thoughts my chest ran sweat under those frozen bushes, and we had hardly reached our place and squatted, peering under branches past the bottoms of the hills set there like giant grey hoofs when through the morning air rang the signal. The warcry of Siksika, The People.

As in that instant before a man's hands meet to clap again, there is silence. It all seems so peaceful, the sound of singing women and children, horses, just hanging there as if not yet quite gone and everything motionless and so quiet with the sunlight dancing on the snow, smoke going straight up from lodges against the river hills and into the blue sky. Then! A roar as 30 men leap up, teeth glistening into sunlight, screaming as we run, stretched out toward our enemies with our knives and plumes and spears pointing the way A-a ha he ha, A-a ha he ha, I yo ho i yo ho, Ha koc e mat, Spum o kit, Spum o kit, I yo ho, i yo ho, our voices thunder in the joy of it as lodges split themselves before our sharp knives and the enemy staggers out snatching at weapons and falling, snatching and falling and trying to stand up! Arrows hiss some of us down but who sees that, we are forcing them back, they are summer flies, their clubs and knives just flies brushed aside and crushed I yo ho the joy of knife thudding in bone and blood spray I yo ho I am here now! And we hear our brothers' voices bellowing toward us above the screams and smoke and know we will meet soon to grasp their bloody hands A-a ha he ha.

But listen! There is a far sound above the roar, the screams, there, between the lodges, the white dust of snow rising with the thunder of hooves down the valley, back back! Back! Each desperate voice cries to each, back! for the open jaws of horses swirl up toward us through the snow of their running with spears and knives and warcries of our enemies bristling above them, shout to your brother that death is running us, back. "All stay together!" Kristo-koom-epoka cries, and we gain the coulee's shelter fast, and we still feel there may be hope but we must turn to face those charging horses.

You see, my friend, this is how it was. In the bend of the Great River below that small camp we attacked, where we could not see it, was the main Cree camp. So big a thousand warriors could jump up in a moment. Appino-kommit knew that early in the morning the horses are always in a camp, and he knew that if we attacked at that time it would save us the trouble of rounding them up. So the thousand warriors in that big camp he didn't know about had to take no more than one running step before they could gallop.

We could tell by the sound of guns that the Cree had six or seven, and we altogether had two, that the others led by Appino-kommit were also retreating to the coulees of the river hills and we would have to get together to stand, if possible. I have told you, my friend, that we wore only breechcloths and moccasins, but that is not true; I also had a shirt I'd got the fall before from the traders in the north at Big House when we got those two guns. It was cotton and only reached my belt but it was a great comfort to me as you will see. Ai he ha, I see it all now, the rush for our lives to the coulee, we reach it and turn just in time to stop them with arrows and a desperate charge against those horses' swinging heads with axes. Ahhh, they are so tight now stabbing around us that horses can be killed with knives, they jam the coulee so tight in their rage to trample us into the frozen ground. They charge again, and again, wheel away and charge again, and four times we meet them on foot, leaping among the foaming horses and smashing knees, smashing them down, our knives driving between ribs and

22

gulping blood straight from pounding hearts I yo ho I ho ho I am here now! The dead piled up in that coulee so high we can't see over them, the bright sunshine and the red circles on the snow as the Cree whirl around once more, and charge again. I can taste my own blood in my mouth here they come again, the fourth charge and I hear their roar as they hurdle the dead and we meet Ha koc e mat! and I am among the horses, my enemy's arm lunging a spear past me and I have that arm, he starts to fall down toward my face and I step slightly aside, knife straight up and it is gone in him to the hilt. The horse rears, screaming, and I twist my knife out, up, and with both hands drive one long red line down through his white and bay belly while he is still on his hind legs pawing above me and his warm curled intestines pour out in one great steaming puddle about his hoofs in the red snow. That hot smell now! Down, he is down like a spilled mountain and the club of a friend spatters his rider's brains in my face and we roar with laughter. They are gone. Gasping I pull another friend from under a floundered horse.

A voice is behind me, Kristo-koom-epoka has to tell me his name for my breath roars in my ears and he is unrecognizable, as if poured over red. "Take cover," he shouts, "they'll come on foot now, with bows! Cover." And they do that, but we are sheltered by the coulee, they have to shoot high into the air and the arrows falling down straight hurt only a few.

"Friends," the voice of Kristo-koom-epoka again, "I don't think anyone wants to stay here; this place is mostly cold and falling arrows. We should go back in threes, two strong take one wounded between them, I'll go first. That way we can get back to the others. Keep close together, come now."

Like a wounded grizzly we started. In an instant our enemy answered our warcry and rushed to meet us. That wasn't the kind of fight a warrior likes to remember, carrying his wounded friend and trying to cut his way out; no joy, no joy. I only remember that as soon as we started an arrow killed the

23

wounded friend I was helping to carry and I took his axe in my right hand and my knife in my left and pushed toward the front to Kristo-koom-epoka. We stood side by side and I helped him to chop our path through Cree. How long that was I don't know, but at last they drew back with only a few arrows spitting at us. We could see then not far away our other party slowly retreating and carrying the wounded as we were. The Cree tried to keep us apart, but up there on the flats they seemed to have worn off their fierceness against our knives and the terrible cold; soon we were together with what was left of our friends. About then some late Cree arrived and put more heart in the enemy, but now we were prepared for them. Appino-kommit sent all the wounded ahead and formed a rear-guard of the strongest that were left. And on the flat plain there and the one shallow line of a beginning coulee we fought for a long time, driving them back again and again until the sun was low. It was the middle of winter, but it took the sun a long time to get there. Then Appino-kommit said to me:

"You are a great runner and your legs are still good. Run ahead of us to the place where we were camped this morning. Tell anyone you find there we must meet in the tall timber we passed through last night, down in that bend. Then you go ahead there and build big fires, the Cree have all our clothing. Run, or many more will die in this cold."

So I left them and I ran. I passed the wounded ones, giving them my message. I ran till there was only one track in the snow and a narrow line of blood for me to follow.

Soon I saw someone running in front of me, not steadily but as if drunk and as I overtook him I looked into his face. He was a boy of fifteen. A shot close in had blown his lower jaw away and his tongue was frozen on his breast with long icicles of saliva and blood. I only looked once and said nothing but ran on. I saw what rode his shoulder. Soon he would go slower, and then he would stop and lie down in the snow, and then sleep. Even now sometimes in a dream I see how he looked at me as I passed him, running without bad wounds, and could not stop to help. I saw him, and the lives of all depended on me, but he did not know that or what I saw, and his look told me that he would feel it even when he couldn't feel his wounds any more. The heat of battle was gone and we were retreating; we had to get to fires; we had to tie up the wounded.

As I ran my heart wanted to die because I had to think of all that faced us. Without clothing, home and safety five long nights and days away, and we had no food. Would our wounded need us after one night of this cold? Of course the Cree would track us, and get the scalps of those who fell, and they would make sure that no-one survived the cold; but they would be all the happier if we froze like dogs rather than on their knives with our warcry sounding. Do you wonder my heart was stretched out?

The sun was cut in half when I reached the grove where the fires were to be built, and there I found some comfort because four sweat lodges made of raw buffalo hides stood under the trees. These could give shelter to some wounded, they would gradually warm if we built large fires outside them, and the hair could be used to stuff the mouths of wounds. If any still bled in the terrible cold. After I had started the first big fire I scraped hair from one of the robes, tied my shirtsleeves tight and pulled my belt very tight around the bottom of my shirt. Then I stuffed hair inside, and I can still feel the warmth that came over me as I worked hard, doing this. And soon people began to arrive, the hurt ones first, and among them Otat-to-ye, the brother of the girl whose shadow I often tried to follow in my dreams. Any child could see he would not reach home. Blood oozed from a hole in his chest and froze on his skin; an arrow had cut through his entrails and its head was buried in his backbone. Only his great heart had brought him this far ai-ha-ha-ha, our hearts so heavy.

No-one said a word as we worked to staunch running blood, to tie sticks around crushed limbs. At last Appino-kommit, with the rearguard. I looked around in the firelight to see who was there, and nearly half of those who had run east under these trees so happily were now lying somewhere in the trampled snow. And of the ones here, over half were badly wounded. But as I looked around I had more courage; in every face burned fierce resolution and revenge; o the early summer sun, may these Cree live long enough to see that! And before dawn our trek had to begin, the strong helping the weak, and those who had died at night we placed in a line against trees facing where the enemy would come so that they could, even in death, glare at the enemy they hated now more than ever.

I and a freind went to Otat-to-ye and lifted him to his feet and, each of us with an arm about him, held his arm over our shoulder with the other hand. We had moved this way only a few steps when he asked us to take him back and place him on the ground beside the dead fire. We did that. Then he said, "Take half of my breechcloth and cover my face." I did that; then he said, "Go fast, the Cree will soon be here, go fast and don't look back."

As we went I heard his voice again, I could barely hear it calling my name. He said as I stood by him again, "Take the cloth off." I did. "Kiss me," he said then, and I did. His eyes were wide open and so black I could look through them and through his skull and see the inside of blackness. "Now put the cloth back, I don't want to see them." And I walked from him again, and I heard nothing behind me.

Friend, can you know how I felt? Do you know pain? That was what made us men, then, such happiness and such pain, that could turn quickly as a hand turning. Our hearts had to know and hold both, and though we were very young we were the children of this land and sky and we did not cry out and make women of ourselves by groaning and cutting ourselves. We were already cut enough; our hearts could bleed in silence. I see by your face you understand some of this; the story I would have to tell his sister, that I had left him alone to wait

26

for their knives because I could not kill him. All day they ran our flanks like wolf shadows on the snow and happy the man whom the wolves got before they, our enemy. And as the sun sank Appino-kommit came and said I would have to run again. I would have to be the one to go ahead and tell all this to our camp, and ask that food and clothing be sent.

Now you will understand about a man bringing such a story to the great camp of our people. When sorrow strikes so swift and hard sometimes a hand flies up and kills the messenger who has dared to speak such words; friend or stranger, it doesn't mater, our love for our own is so strong. As soon as it was dark I started. It was colder and the snow had begun to drift before a northwest wind and I had to run against that all night. I rested a little when I could not twist my strength any tighter, then all the next day, taking only a short sleep by a fire in the middle of the day, then on for three days and nights. In the evening of the third day I came near our great camp; I had eaten only rose-bush berries as I ran and slept no more than half a night altogether, watching for what might be following me, and I could barely walk as I came in, my face frozen and legs cut by the crusted snow. I moved toward the chief's lodge, for only there was there safety for me, but children recognized me and ran through the camp crying that one had come back alone who could scarcely walk and had gone to the chief's lodge. The whole camp ran together.

I entered the lodge and seated myself under the Medicine, and I will tell you what that means, my friend, for you will not know it. The door of a lodge is always toward the rising sun and the chief's bed is always exactly opposite the door, that is, against the back side of the lodge equal distance from the door if you go either to the right or the left when you enter, and the head of the bed is always to the north so that when the chief sits during the day his face is always east toward his own fire in the centre of his lodge and the rising sun. There are reasons for this. At the head of the bed on his left is a tripod, his robe

27

rests on one side of this and under the tripod he keeps his war bonnet, his tobacco, and the other sacred things, and over this, but outside the lodge, hangs his Medicine. Now whoever comes in and sits down on his left before the tripod also sits under the Medicine, and even if he is the enemy, if he gets to the middle of the camp where the chief's lodge is and gets inside and gains that place, he is safe as long as he remains there. Once out of that place anyone may kill him, if he hasn't convinced them otherwise. So I got in, and got under the Medicine, sitting there in the warm, safest place of my people with my head hanging to my knees, and I couldn't say anything as the people ran together outside.

For a long time the chief sat with his head bowed. He had not said a word when I jerked open his lodge door so naked and bloody, and he said nothing while the sounds of people outside grew and one by one the councillors came in silently and looked at me and seated themselves on my left. At last the chief reached behind him for his tobacco board and prepared a pipe of tobacco and slowly filled his great pipe. He passed the pipe to one councillor, who placed the stem in his mouth, turning the bowl toward another and that one took a live coal from the fire and placed it on the tobacco. When it was lit, the councillor passed the pipe back to the chief. He pointed the smoking stem toward the rising sun and prayed to The Great God, to the sun, stars and moon, to earth and sky and water, that they have pity on his people. Then he passed the pipe to me; he bid me smoke, and called his women to prepare food. When I had smoked and eaten in silence the chief took my hand and said,

"Do any live?"

"Yes."

He repeated my answer to the people.

"Are they in danger?"

"Yes, from starvation and wounds."

"How far are they?"

"In two days they should be here, those still alive."

Again he cried this out to the people, and orders were given that warriors take food and robes to them.

And then began the hardest of all. The people began to ask about their loved ones. One would enter the lodge and call a name and I would make the sign for living; then rejoicing would echo in the warm lodge and all around it from those outside, but perhaps at the next name called I would have to make the sign of death, or wounded, and the sounds of mourning began and soon there was nothing but that sound surrounding me. I could not lift my head under it and I heard my mother's voice asking about her youngest son, three times she asked and I couldn't answer, I had no power left to lift my hand, there was nothing left in me hearing her voice for my father was dead and she was already bent under great sorrows. But I made that sign too. And the wails grew and still I made the dreaded sign and still I heard that one voice, the one I loved and so dreadful now on and on until my heart gave way. I sprang to my feet, shouting, "Don't ask me for Otat-to-ye, don't ask! How can I say his last word beside the dead fire?" And when I had said that I heard a low cry in front of me and the world turned black. When I knew something again two days later they told me 50 young men had been brought back. The relief party reached them just in time, or not ten would have returned. 50 out of 300.

It is late my friend, and time to sleep. That was our life then, that was what made us men, such happiness and glory and pain that could turn quickly as a hand turning. When the Old Men still taught us and we lived with the great buffalo and the rivers on this land which had been given to our fathers before us and we had the strength to breathe and run wherever our eye moved across the land under this sky. Yes, we wailed that winter in the cold valleys of the Red Deer, and the Cree, Ai he ha, the Cree that summer! You see, white traders finally dared come closer to us because we were friendly and we piled our robes up against their guns and the longest of them could kill farther than any gun I ever saw. No, he was too young, it was Ok-ki-kit-sip-pe-me-o-tas the war chief who led us. And how the Crees wailed that summer along the Great River, ahhh, how they wailed.

The White Mustang

Edward A. McCourt

I

The boy had run all the way from the upland pasture and his thin eager face was damp with sweat. His father was standing at the shady end of the barn sharpening a mower knife, and the grating noise of granite drawn over steel sounded loud in the afternoon stillness. The boy stopped directly in front of his father, shoved his hands deep into the pockets of his faded blue denim overalls and spat in the dust that lay thick around his bare feet. Some saliva dribbled over his chin and he quickly wiped it away with the back of his hand, hoping that his father had not noticed. "Dad—what do you think I saw way up on the hog's-back?"

His father held the mower knife upright and began methodically testing the triangular blades with his thumb. "What, Jed?"

"A horse—a grey horse! I figger maybe it's the one the Judsons lost and Mr. Judson said he'd give $5 reward to anyone who found him! Gee, Dad, can't I ride up and see? If I got the $5 I'd be able to send for the .22 in the catalogue. It only costs $6.35 delivered and I've got a dollar and a half now."

The words burst out with a kind of explosive force that left the boy breathless and red in the face. He inhaled deeply, making a sucking noise, and scuffed the dirt with his bare feet. His father picked up the sharpening stone and eyed it critically.

"Not today, son," he said. "It's a long way up to the hog's-back on a hot day like this."

Jed turned away and looked at the big poplars down by the creek and tried not to think of anything at all. "But maybe tomorrow," his father said. "You could start right after breakfast. Only—"

"Gee, Dad—that'll be great! I could be back for dinner easy."

"Only you see, Jed, I can't figure how Judson's horse could have got up to the hog's-back. Not from their side anyway. It's a mighty steep climb and there's no grass to lead a horse on. You're sure you saw one up top?"

"Gee, yes, Dad, just as plain as anything—standing right on the skyline. Honest it was a horse. Grey, nearly white I guess, just like the Judsons'. I was 'bout half a mile up in the pasture picking strawberries when I saw him."

His father leaned the mower-knife against the wall of the barn. As if a cord holding them in place had suddenly given way, his long limbs relaxed and he collapsed on the ground, his back miraculously against the wall of the barn, his legs straight out in front of him. From his overalls' pocket he pulled out a blackened pipe, held it between thumb and forefinger and looked at it without saying anything. Then his eyes crinkled at the corners.

"Son, I don't figure that was the Judson horse you saw at all."

Jed knew that his father was playing a game. Dermot O' Donnell loved to play games. Jed laughed out loud and sprawled in the dust at his father's feet. "Then whose horse was it?"

"No-one's, Jed. You've seen the white mustang."

"What white mustang, Dad?"

Dermot's heavy eyebrows shot up and threatened to disappear into his hairline. "Child, child, what do they teach you in school anyway? Nothing that matters or you'd have heard of the white mustang!"

He tamped down the tobacco in his pipe and struck a match

along the left leg of his overalls, all the time wagging his head slowly from side to side. "There's hardly a puncher in the plains country clear from the Rio Grande to Calgary who hasn't seen the white mustang at one time or another. Mostly at night of course, when the moon is shining and he looks more silver than white. You can get closer to him too, but not very close at that. But sometimes you see him in the daytime, only way off, and he doesn't stand long then."

"And has nobody ever caught him?"

"Not yet, Jed. You see, he's no ordinary horse. Seems like he never gets any older. And some fools have shot at him, but they either missed or the bullets went right through him and did no hurt at all. Anyway, no-one has ever even slowed him up. And you can't catch him on horseback. Once, so they tell me, they took after him in relays—down in the Texas Panhandle it was—and chased him three days without a stop. But the white mustang never turned a hair. At the end of the three days two horses were dead and a lot more windbroken for life. But they never got within a half a mile of the mustang and every so often he'd turn around and laugh at them the way a horse does if he's feeling extra good. Last I heard he was down in Wyoming working north. Way I figure it, no ordinary horse could get up the hog's-back from the Judson side. I guess it's the white mustang all right."

"Will you give me $5 if I catch him?"

"$5 is it? $5?" The pain in Dermot's voice was almost real. "Jed, if you ever catch the white mustang, you'll find him tame as a turtle-dove. And when you get on his back he'll take you away—just like flying it'll be, I think—to a country you've never seen where the grass is as green as the spring feathers of a mallard. And in a little glen so close to the sea you can hear the waves wash on the rocks, you'll find a beautiful princess with long golden hair waiting for you. And she'll get up behind you and put her arms around your middle and the white mustang will bring you back like he's a flash of lightning. And

33

I'll build a house for you and the princess in the poplars down by the creek, and the two of you will be able to help your mother and me. And all your children—you'll have a grand houseful of them in no time—will learn to ride on the back of the white mustang, and when their time comes they'll ride away on him to be kings and queens all over the world. But mind you, Jed, no-one has ever yet laid a rope on the white mustang."

Jed spoke thoughtfully. "I think I'd sooner have $5."

Jed's father was the most wonderful man in the world and his laughter was the most wonderful part of him. He laughed now, silently at first, then in a series of staccato explosions that culminated in a sustained gargantuan bellow. Jed laughed too; he always did, listening to his father. Then he ran away and lay down on his back in the middle of the grove of poplars where his father was going to build the house for the princess, and looked up through the tree-tops at the blue sky and thought of the things he would do with the .22 rifle.

2

Jed did not ride up to the hog's-back the next day. For the heatwave broke in a drenching rain that began as a thunderstorm over the mountains and spread out across the foothills in a steady, settled downpour. Jed tried not to show his disappointment. He knew that the rain was needed badly, that without it his father's small crop, already stunted and parched and clinging precariously to life, would have been burnt beyond hope of recovery in a week or less. But such considerations were theoretic and remote, of small weight beside the immediate loss of a day's adventure and $5 at the end of it.

Late in the afternoon Jed put on the high rubber boots and oil slicker which were among his most prized possessions and climbed up the path through the pasture and beyond until he was no more than a mile from the hog's-back, an immense arching hill-top that seemed as remote as a mountain-peak and almost as inaccessible. There was no path beyond the fenced upland pasture, and the long slope above was steep and treacherous underfoot. Jed had been up to the hog's-back only once; his father had taken him there one cool spring day, and the memory of what he had seen from the summit was like a lovely haunting dream. Now that he had been granted permission to go alone, the delay seemed to eat at his stomach and leave a hollow ache unlike any other pain he had ever known. Once, when he looked up, the swirling mists far up the slope seemed to part for a moment, and he glimpsed a whiteness that was no part of the elements. It was a whitness that you didn't see in horses very ofteh, and its outlines, vague and indistinct though they were, suggested the existence of something strange, portentous behind the wavering curtain of mist. Then the clouds closed in again and there were no more breaks. At last, when the rain had penetrated his slicker at a dozen points and was running in cold rivulets down his back, Jed turned away and half walked, half slithered down through a tangle of undergrowth to the comparative level of the pasture below.

He was quiet at supper that night. His mother had made his favourite dish of beef stew with puffy white dumplings floating in the gravy, and for a while there was no time to talk. But when the dessert came—pie made of dried apples and Saskatoon berries—Jed stopped with the first mouthful impaled on his fork and looked at his father. "Dad, is the white mustang very big?"

Dermot chewed a mouthful of food and swallowed. "Not big, Jed. A mustang is never big. But he looks big—like everything that's uncommon. Take Napoleon now. You'd measure him for a uniform and he was a small man, a runt—not much over five feet, I guess. And then you'd stand back and take a look at him and he was big. He was the biggest man you ever saw." That was another thing about Dermot—he made you feel that he had known Napoleon very well in the old days. Or

35

Robin Hood or Brian Boru, or whoever he happened to be talking about.

Jed's mother filled Dermot's cup to the brim with strong black tea.

"What nonsense are you stuffing the boy's head with now, Dermot?" she asked. She was a small frail woman, the physical antithesis of her husband. But there was the same look in her dark eyes, a kind of remoteness in them that made her concern for the immediate seem casual at best.

"No nonsense, Mother, no nonsense at all. He hears enough of that at school."

"I wouldn't say that in front of the boy, Dermot," she said. "Maybe he'll learn enough at school to help him keep one foot on the solid earth. Dear knows it's more than he'll ever learn at home."

But she spoke without malice. And she looked at Dermot and Jed in a way that seemed to make no difference between them.

Next morning the sun shone from a clear sky and the mists rose from the earth in steaming exhalations that vanished before the cool wind blowing from the north-west. The ground underfoot was soft and spongy—muddy where there was no grass—and the grass itself washed clean of dust so that it looked as if it had turned green again overnight. Jed dressed quickly and hurried into the kitchen for breakfast. "It's a swell day, Dad," he said.

His father set a pail full of milk on the shelf in the little pantry adjoining the kitchen. "A fine day indeed, Jed. And I know what's in your mind. But I'll have to take Paddy and ride out to the far pasture this morning to look for the yearlings. They didn't come up with the cows and I'm thinking the fence may be down. But you'll be able to make hog's-back this after-noon. It'll be a cool day I think."

Jed did not protest the delay. He knew what his father was thinking, that the grey horse would be gone anyway and that half a day would make no difference. He swallowed the lump in his throat and ate breakfast quietly but without appetite. After breakfast, when Dermot had ridden off down the valley to the far pasture in the flats, he amused himself snaring gophers in the little patch of wheat just across the creek. But it was not a pastime he ever really enjoyed. He got a thrill from seeing the grey-brown head pop up from the hole in the earth —from the quick savage pull that trapped the victim—from the feel of weight at the end of the long line of binder-twine as he swung it through the air. But what had to be done afterwards was not so pleasant. Particularly he hated taking the string from the neck of the battered carcass, covered with blood and insides as it so often was. This morning his attempts were half-hearted and mostly unsuccessful. After a while he threw his string away and returned to the house. He felt hungry, and there were cookies in the big green tin on the bottom shelf of the cupboard, and milk in the earthenware jug that always stood in the coolness of the cellar steps. He poured out a cup of milk, sat down at the table and ate his way steadily through a plateful of cookies. His mother was busy at the small worktable by the window. Jed finished his last mouthful of cookie and pushed back his chair.

"Mom?"

"What is it, Jed?"

"Mom, did you ever hear about the white mustang?"

"Only what your father told you." Mrs. O'Donnell lifted a pie from the oven, using a corner of her ample gingham apron to protect her hands from the heat, and set it on the worktable. She stood beside the table looking out of the window, and her voice was so low that Jed could hardly hear her.

"Your grandmother used to tell me a story about a white horse. The son of Finn rode away on him to a fairyland where he lived with a beautiful princess. They called her Naim the Golden-Haired. But he got lonely and rode back on the white horse to his own country. He knew that he shouldn't get off the white horse, but he wanted to feel the turf under his feet. And the white horse ran away and the son of Finn turned into an old man. That's what happens to people when they come back to earth."

Jed emptied his cup and set it on the table. "It's a funny thing, Mom. An awful lot of people believe in the white horse, don't they?"

His mother turned from the window without speaking. After a while Jed went back outside. He walked part way up the path to the pasture, then cut across to where the creek, rising from a spring far up in the hills, ran over rocks and gravel to the valley below. He sat on a flat rock and let the water trickle over his bare feet. The water was cold, but he liked the sensation of numbness stealing through his feet— first the instep, then the toes, heels last of all. Even better he liked the prickling feel of returning warmth when he drew his feet out of the water and warmed them on the surface of the rock. He stayed there a long time, until he heard his mother's high "coo-ee" and knew that it was time for dinner.

Dermot was late getting home. So late that Mrs. O'Donnell put his dinner away in the warming oven of the big range and brewed a fresh pot of tea. Jed waited stoically; but when he saw his father approaching up the valley trail he shouted at the top of his lungs and ran down to open the gate for him.

"Gee, Dad, I thought you were never going to get here!"

Dermot slid down from the saddle and stretched prodigiously.

"It was just as I thought—fence down and the yearlings miles away. Paddy's had a hard morning."

"He's too fat," Jed said. "He'll be all right in a little while."

He emptied a tin pail of oats into the manger feed-box while Dermot unsaddled the sweating pony. They went into the house together without saying anything. Mrs. O'Donnell was setting Dermot's dinner on the table. "You're late, Dermot," she said.

38

"I am late, Mother. And I'm thinking it would be as well if Jed waited till morning now. Paddy needs a couple of hours' rest at least. And the grey horse is sure to be far away by this time."

Mrs. O'Donnell spoke with unusual sharpness. "Paddy can have his rest and there still will be plenty of time. The evenings are long and the boy will be home before dark."

Jed's heart gave a great leap. His father grinned at him. "And they tell you it's the womenfolk are over-anxious about their young," was all he said.

3

It was after two o'clock when Jed went to the barn to saddle Paddy. He threw the heavy stock-saddle over Paddy's broad back and pulled the cinch. You had to pretend you were all finished so the little sorrel would relax his distended belly. Then you gave the cinch-strap a quick sharp pull and took in about three inches of slack. As soon as the saddle was securely in place Jed shortened the stirrups and tied a lasso to the cantle. He could not throw a lasso very well, and anyway the Judson horse was a quiet nag that could be led on a halter-shank. But the lasso looked impressive, and it was a good idea always to be ready for anything.

He rode Paddy to the water-trough and let him drink a few mouthfuls. His mother came to the door and he waved to her and she waved back and smiled. "Don't be late, Jed."

"I won't," he shouted. "So long, Mom!"

For nearly an hour he rode upward without pause, the pony stumbling often in the damp uncertain footing. The valley slid farther and farther away below him until at last Jed was able to see over the opposite side to the great plain itself. He stopped at last, not because he wanted to but Paddy was blowing heavily. He dropped to the ground and squatted on his haunches while Paddy stood quietly beside him with bowed head. Jed could no longer see his own house because of an intervening swell in the seemingly regular contour of the hillside, but other houses had come into view—Joe Palamiro's shack near where the valley ran out into the plain, and the Peterson place, easily identified because of the big windmill, right at the edge of the plain itself. And he could see, far out on the plain, a row of tall gaunt red buildings—grain elevators—standing like guardsmen on parade, and beyond them a second row, over the horizon itself, so that only the upper halves of the elevators were visible. Another time Jed would have been tempted to linger, trying to identify familiar landmarks when seen from an unfamiliar angle. But now, after only a minute or two, he stirred restlessly. Paddy tossed his head and began to nibble at a few tufts of grass growing around the base of a boulder. Jed leapt to his feet.

"All right, you old geezer," he said. "If you can eat you can travel. I'll lead you for awhile."

He unfastened the halter-shank from the saddle-horn and started up the hill on foot, Paddy crowding close behind. There was no trace of path anywhere and Jed had to pick his steps with care along deep dry gulches channelled by the rush of water in springtime, over glacial deposits of shale and boulder, past dwarfed poplars and evergreen. There were flowers blooming on these upper slopes that he had never seen before, but he couldn't stop to look at them. In spite of the uncertain footing he went up quickly. The sweat gathered on his forehead and ran down his face in salty trickles, for the sun was hot now and the wind had almost completely died away. But the hog's-back was close at hand; already Jed could distinguish objects on the skyline—a stunted bush, a pile of rocks forming a natural cairn, a single tree as incongruous in its lonely setting as a human figure would have been.

Now that he was almost at the top Jed suddenly and unaccountably wanted to linger. For the second time he sat down and looked back. Below, the scene had spread out and yet diminished. The horizon had moved farther back; now he was high enough to catch a glimpse of distant emerald green where a river flowed between enormous banks, of towns so remote that it was impossible to conceive of their having actual being. They were mirages that would vanish with the shimmering heat waves that now hung above the level of the plain. Objects which half an hour ago had seemed close at hand—Joe Palamiro's shack and the Peterson windmill and the upright slab of granite at the mouth of the valley called, for no reason anyone knew of, the Dead Man's Needle—had somehow contracted, and slipped away as if carried on the surface of an outgoing tide. Jed sat for a long time until Paddy, dissatisfied with scanty pickings, came close and nuzzled his shoulder.

"All right, all right," Jed said. "We'll be moving."

He mounted and rode on. The ground was bare and brownish grey. Not even the drenching rain of the day previous could restore life to the few wisps of dry grass that lingered near the top, or the tall reedy stems of upland foxgloves that rattled mournfully in the wind again blowing across the foothills. His father was right, the boy thought, there was no feed up here for a horse. A horse like the Judson grey, he said to himself, in unthinking qualification.

And when he reached the very top at last and was able to look down the opposite side—down a slope that was strange and steep and menacing although he had seen it once before and it had not seemed menacing then—he remembered what his father had said about the inaccessibility of the hog's-back from the Judson side. Dermot was right. No horse could climb that slope. No horse would want to. Jed felt no regret but instead an unexpected lightness of spirit, a strange confusion of happiness and something that made him a little bit afraid. For he had seen a horse on the hog's-back—a horse more white than grey. He laughed out loud, then looked quickly at the sun. It was swinging low toward the mountains. It would be twilight in an hour and the dark would come soon afterwards.

He rode along the hog's-back until checked by the precipitous side of a dry gully, then returned to the highest point of the arching hill-top, and again looked down the great slope that fell away to the west. The world that looked different, hill rising above hill until at last they broke into the scintillating splendour of white peaks against a pale blue sky. For no reason at all Jed wanted to cry. Instead he shouted loudly at Paddy and drove his heels into the pony's fat sides.

Paddy trotted a few steps and slowed to a walk. It was then that Jed saw the trees. They were directly below him, just over the first big curve of the west slope. At first he could see only their tops, but as he went down they came completely into view—stunted Balm-of-Gileads that looked curiously unreal in their symmetrical grouping on the barren hillside. And low down, between two grey-green trunks, Jed could see a patch of white.

He rode forward at a walk. Paddy snorted once and Jed pulled hard on the reins. He wanted to turn and ride back up the slope and over the summit toward home. But instead he went on slowly, and the dead weight that dragged at his heart made him faint and sick. He reached the circle of trees. Paddy could smell the water now, although the wind was blowing the other way, and snorted again. But Jed said "no" very quietly and with a funny quaver in his voice. He could see the white patch clearly now, above the surface of the water and partly on the ground. And he could hear the heavy buzzing noise made by the swollen blue-bottles as they rose in clouds from the carcass of the grey horse that had died—quickly or slowly, it did not matter now—in the treacherous sucking mud surrounding the hillside spring.

Paddy, scenting death, pawed the ground and whinnied. Jed swung the pony hard and slapped him with the ends of the reins. "Giddap-giddap!" he shouted. He rode over the hog's-back at a gallop and on down the other side. Paddy stumbled and almost fell. Jed pulled him in with a savage jerk.

"All right, you old geezer," he said. "Take it easy. No need to break your neck."

It was almost dark when Jed reached home. His father and mother were in the yard waiting for him. "I was on the point of starting after you," Dermot shouted, "when we saw you up there like a god against the setting sun." And he laughed a great booming laugh that echoed across the valley.

His mother kissed him on the cheek. "Your father will put Paddy away, Jed," she said. "I've kept your supper hot for you."

Jed washed very carefully and combed his hair. He had to comb it several times before he got the part right. His mother lit the oil-lamp and set it on the table.

"You must be starved, Jed," she said. "I've got a lovely supper for you. Bacon and eggs and the strawberries you picked the day before yesterday."

Dermot came stamping into the kitchen. "And did you lay eyes on the white mustang, son?"

For a minute Jed did not answer. "He's dead," he said at last. "It was Judson's grey. He got bogged in a spring."

Astonishment showed in Dermot's face. "So you did see him day before yesterday! But how ever did he get up?"

"There's a stream running down from the spring. He must have followed it up. The grass would be good along the banks."

Dermot filled his pipe. "Too bad, son," he said.

He lit his pipe and blew such clouds of smoke that for a minute his face was almost hidden. "I figure, Jed," he said, somehow talking like one man to another, "that tomorrow you and I had better take a little trip to town."

Jed looked at his father quickly. Dermot blew another cloud of smoke. "The gophers are getting pretty bad. Doesn't seem like we'll be able to keep them down at all unless you get a .22. There's one in Heath's Hardware—nice little single-shot —for $7. I figure we can maybe swing it."

"Gee, Dad," Jed said, "that'll be great."

Suddenly he pushed away his plate. "Mom," he said, "I'm not hungry."

His mother laid her hand on his shoulder. "Would you like to go to bed?" she said.

Jed got up and turned away so his father could not see his face. He nodded jerkily. His mother spoke to Dermot.

"He's tired out. He'll be all right in the morning."

They went out to the little porch where Jed slept in the summertime. The night air was warm and still and full of rich scents that you didn't notice in daytime. The moon had risen and a band of silver lay across the top of the valley wall opposite. Jed began to cry, silently. His mother put her arms around him without speaking and held him tight.

The door opened and Dermot came out to the porch. "Look at him, would you?" he said, and there was a petulant note in his voice. "All this fuss about a dead horse."

Jed's mother looked at Dermot. When she spoke he could hardly hear her. "Not just a horse, Dermot," she said. "Not an ordinary horse anyway."

And she repeated, matter-of-factly, "He's tired out. He'll be all right in the morning."

Dermot stared at her for a long minute in silence. Then he nodded soberly. "Sure, Mother," he said. "He'll be all right in the morning."

And he closed the door so quietly behind him that it made no noise at all.

Mahigan's Atonement

Georges Bugnet

I

In a valley of the Athabasca there lies an oval lake, extending east and west. On a certain December day, it was already frozen over and covered with that dazzling, velvety mantle that the first snow lays over the closed waters and the sleeping earth. The pale gold of the winter sun streamed down upon it. Its shores, on all sides, were thickly peopled with century-old trees—willows, poplars, birches, larches, black spruces and occasional pines—all standing straight and motionless, petrified in the frozen silence.

Yet, at intervals, as the cold grew more or less intense, the ice contracted or expanded with cracklings and rumblings, followed by musical vibrations that rippled over the surface and spread through the entire valley. At other times, the shrill howl of a coyote rent the air, rebounding from solitude to solitude and dying away in the far-off silences.

In the middle of this lake there is an oblong islet, steep and rocky, its sides hollowed out by the waves except at the southern end, where the softer rock has crumbled. Its flat top, swept bare by the winds, gives it the appearance of an ancient altar, a dolmen erected on a desert plain. On that December day, it looked so dark against the whiteness, so grim in its isolation, that it was as a stain on a white robe, or as a sin on a pure soul. The Indians, believing it to be haunted by the Evil Spirit, had called it "The Islet of Mati-Manito" (the Sneaky Spirit).

But Kitse-Manito, the Great Spirit, Who is everywhere,

Who sees everything, Who knows everything, looked upon His work and saw that it was good.

2

From the east side of the lake a black speck moved toward the islet, gradually growing taller and trailing a long shadow on the snow, for the sun was already low on the horizon.

It was Mahigan.

On his back was a pack containing his trapping outfit. His right hand, swinging rhythmically, carried a gun. He wore a large fur cap, purchased at the Hudson's Bay post nearby, and his small, dark eyes were gleaming beneath its glossy rim; neither the sun, shining full in his face, nor the blinding dazzle of the snow could alter the peculiar fixity of his gaze. His bronzed cheekbones, flat nose, and thick lips protruded above his thin, stubby, black beard. His garments were of that light, pliant, whitish leather that results when unsmoked moose-hide is properly tanned. His cuffs, sleeves and collar, elaborately trimmed with red and blue arabesques of dyed and plaited hairs, seemed alive, owing to the flutterings of very fine leather fringes. Three rows of tiny glass beads of different colours glittered on his moccasins. In his belt was an axe.

At the foot of the islet, Mahigan laid down his pack and gun. With his knife, he cut a red-barked shoot of kinikinik, peeled off the coarsest part of the bark, and carefully scraped the thin cambium layer into the palm of his hand. To this he added a pinch of dry tobacco—a matter of taste and economy. When he had lit his pipe with slow, luxurious puffs, he went to look at his traps.

This was a very good place for muskrats. In summer, the low grassy shore was thickly covered with the reeds and rushes that this animal uses to fashion its nest; also, the islet's sinister reputation kept other trappers at a distance. As for Mahigan, he had no fear of Mati-Manito.

He had not gone twenty paces when he stopped short. Fresh tracks were visible near the first trap, in which only the rump and tail of a weasel remained.

"Hunhun!"

Mahigan put out his pipe with a pinch of snow, went back for his gun, and then followed those fresh tracks. At the north end of the shore, he suddenly came face to face with the thief, caught in a trap; it was a magnificent silver fox, still alive, and from beneath a clump of willows its eyes gleamed and closed alternately.

"Hunhun! Hunhun!"

This time, Mahigan grasped two facts: it was an unexpected stroke of luck; it was not his. He had never placed a trap in this particular spot. But if he was not afraid of demons, he was even less afraid of man. He dispatched the animal promptly with the back of his axe and hurriedly began stripping off its precious skin.

3

To the south, another black speck had detached itself swiftly from the edge of the brown forest and was running over the white surface of the lake. The newcomer very soon reached the islet; he clambered up the loose rocks and walked along the flat top to the north end. His walk, dress, figure, and face were very like Mahigan's.

Upon reaching the edge of the overhanging cliff, he lay flat on his stomach and, for a moment, watched what was going on down below. Then, in a low, calm voice, he said:

"Mahigan!"

Mahigan started slightly. He paused in his nearly-finished task and looked all around him. Instinctively, he raised his head. He saw the barrel of a rifle pointed right between his eyes and, beyond it, a face with one eye closed and the other gleaming above the sights with curious intentness.

"Mahigan, you have taken what belongs to me. Leave it!"

"Mistatim, this islet is my hunting-ground."

"The land is anybody's. Haven't you put your traps close to mine before? And have I ever touched any of your catches? But you have stolen mine before. That is a low-down trick. We are brothers, with the same father and mother. I have a wife; you haven't."

"You have always had the best luck. . . . It's all right. I am going."

Mahigan got up. With one bound, before the other had decided what to do, he was under the shelter of the overhanging cliff, rifle in hand.

Mistatim drew back. It was his turn to find himself in a tight corner. Under cover of the beetling cliffs, his brother might change his place and attack him unawares from he knew not where, perhaps from behind. He crawled backward and lay flat in the middle of the islet.

Suddenly he heard faint crunchings on the east side. Was his brother making off with the precious fur? Pointing his rifle in that direction, he crawled to the edge and raised himself a little. He scarcely had time to glimpse the silvery pelt hanging from Mahigan's belt and Mahigan himself walking backward, ready to shoot, before a bullet struck his skull, making him give a slight jump. Then he crumpled up at the edge of the cliff, on the snow-covered face of the islet.

And all Nature shuddered at the reverberation of that tragic sound.

After a few minutes, Mahigan approached cautiously, clambered up the rocks at the southern end, and, seeing the motionless form, went and shook it.

"Hunhun!"

He pulled off his victim's fur cap, then replaced it. The bullet had struck the top of his forehead. Blood was trickling onto

48

the snow, staining it with a crimson pool that grew larger and larger, setting a seal of unusually vivid colour on the islet—now more than ever resembling an ancient altar—on the lake with its white, velvety mantle, and on the entire valley, peopled with its grey, century-old trees, petrified in the frozen silence.

Then Mahigan's eyes, which had been so peculiarly steady, began to blink as if in too strong a light. Yet the sun had already gone down behind the far-off western hills, and everything in the valley was growing darker.

Mahigan descended the rocks slowly, put the silvery spoil in his pack, then turned eastward again.

And the Great Spirit, Who is everywhere, Who sees everything, Who knows everything, looked upon His work and saw that it was good.

4

Mahigan was only half-way across the lake when, in the east, a dark figure appeared on its pearl-grey surface, near the edge of the bush.

"Hunhun."

This signified merely perception, not recognition. Mahigan paused for a moment and stared intently.

"Hunhun!"

This time, he had recognized the figure. Having come to a decision, he went on again, and the two shadows glided nearer to each other in the deepening twilight.

"Good evening, my son!"

"Hunhun! Where are you going so late, Father?"

Father Lozée stood still. His strong frame was warmly clad in a brown bearskin. A haversack was slung across his shoulders. Below his beaver cap, his face was round and full and quite pink. His clear, keen eyes, flashing under the grey, bushy eyebrows, looked right through the blinking eyes of Mahigan, into his very soul.

"I am on my way to your brother's. His wife has just given birth to a son and I am going to baptise him."

"Hunhun!"

Mahigan's eyes fell. There was a brief space of deep silence.

"Father, you never repeat what is told to the priest of Kitse-Manito?"

"Never, my son."

"Mistatim will never speak to you again, Father! He wanted to steal my hunting-ground. Mati-Manito urged me, and I killed my brother."

"Where? When?"

"Just now, on the Islet of Mati-Manito. Will my Father grant me the forgiveness of Kitse-Manito?"

"My son, tell me everything. Mistatim was not bad. It is you whom they call a thief. What did you quarrel about? What had you stolen from him?"

"The islet is my hunting-ground."

"Tell me everything, my son. If you have stolen, you must give back. If you have killed, you must repent; you must make amends; you must help his wife; and you must expiate your crime and do penance from this time on."

"Would Kitse-Manito be satisfied with twenty muskrat skins?"

"A hundred muskrat skins would not make up for your crime. Your very heart must weep."

"Would Kitse-Manito be satisfied with two hundred muskrat skins?"

"Mahigan, God has nothing to do with muskrat skins. He desires to see remorse in a bleeding heart."

"Would Kitse-Manito be satisfied with half the value of a silver fox?"

"Ah! So that is what you stole? Wretched slayer of your brother! And still you try to bargain! To a heart such as yours

50

God never grants His pardon. Begone, and never come back until you have repented! Mahigan, it is not possible for any man to sell himself to God!"

5

As Mahigan went on his way, night fell, the night of the Alberta highlands, where shadow is still luminous; a night that comes early and lingers late, rising from the snow-covered plains in the east to the snow-covered plains of the sky; a night when the Aurora Borealis holds carnival, undulating from horizon to horizon, her radiant tresses streaming behind her, translucent and powdered with stars.

When Mahigan reached the edge of the bush, he did not turn round, did not look back at the islet that resembled an ancient altar, but plunged into the leafless gloom and soon afterwards arrived at his log shack.

It stood in the middle of a long clearing where, in an earlier time, fire had destroyed the forest. The snow-covered ground gleamed wanly in the darkness. It bristled with coal-black stumps and was strewn with black-ribbed skeletons over which the snow had laid pale shrouds.

Usually Mahigan did not worry about how things looked, but that night he sat at his door very late. He had no fire, for the soft breath of the Chinook wind was coming from the south-west in slow, warm puffs. Suddenly, he noticed that everything in front of him was taking on a reddish tint; the snow was turning pink: yet the afterglow had faded long before.

Coming from nowhere, something was beginning to fill the starry skies—something like a ghostly emanation, or like the mist that drifts slowly from the mouth of one who sighs in a frozen atmosphere. But this must have been an endless sigh, an extraordinary sigh, for the mist gradually spread across the middle of the heavens, from west to east, and it was red.

Mahigan had never seen this rare phenomenon before. He felt uneasy. What could it mean?

From the pale, transparent red, the mist gradually deepened, particularly in the centre, and formed a long streak almost parallel to the Milky Way. Through this purple mist, in unfathomable depths of deepest violet, the stars twinkled like astonished eyes.

From pale red, the mist rapidly turned bright red, almost scarlet. And how it glowed, palpitated, quivered! It moved as if endowed with life. Shapes crowned with fiery haloes appeared, unrolling themselves majestically, stretching themselves out in wavy lines, separating, commencing to turn in vast, sinuous curves, then breaking up and vanishing like sluggish eddies on the sheen of a broad stream.

At times, they seemed to descend earthward, letting fall a rain of crimson light that bathed the snow in roseate hues. Furtive gleams quivered like sudden, fleeting flashes of lightning in the distance, or the flash of a gun in darkness.

Hosts of weird apparitions, tinged with purple, descended slowly from the zenith of the heavens, unrolled themselves and, breaking up, spread out in vast waves that flooded almost the entire firmament. They emitted what looked like blood-spurts, and these gave birth to monstrous shapes that seemed to dart about, fly from horizon to horizon, then meet and mingle: they appeared and disappeared by turns, like powers of life in conflict with powers of death.

On the ground, near the haggard man, everything was bathed in an unearthly light. The black skeletons had assumed livid hues; the entire clearing seemed inundated by a tide of discoloured blood.

Mahigan, sitting motionless at his shack door, closed his eyes and shuddered. He fancied he saw an islet on that lake of discoloured blood and on top of the islet two mournful eyes in the pale, frozen face of a corpse.

He was not sure, at first, that all this was a threat from Kitse-Manito, but he sensed some formidable power behind it. This feeling grew in intensity until emotion brought conviction. Children and simple-minded people who do not reason things out may reform, if they are bad, through fear of punishment. Mahigan felt in his heart that there was a Supreme Power: he did not feel there was not. That, for him, was sufficient. He could disbelieve no longer. It seemed evident to him that some expiation for his crime was about to be required of him; that his punishment would be meted out by degrees and inexorably. Then, like other souls of stronger mould, who feel their doubts disappear in the face of Death, Mahigan formed a resolve and agreed to a sacrifice. He rose and went into his shack, put the silver fur back in his belt, and picked up his gun. Stoically, without haste, he went back toward the lake.

As if already appeased, the red apparitions gradually lost their bloody tints. Their brightness increased; they turned pink, then white, amber, gold, pale green and mauve. Gliding back to the north, they formed a vast arc, tranquil and watchful. Rays of serene light radiated from it so that it resembled an immense fan.

6

The frozen, snow-covered lake lay bathed in the tranquil, silvery radiance of the northern lights. The century-old trees that peopled its shores had been wakened from their frozen slumber by the warm breath of the Chinook; their tops swayed with musical rustlings; their branches sang softly of this ephemeral resurrection.

In the midst of the icy plain, the silent islet was waiting.

Out of the east, a black speck moved nearer. It was Mahigan. Just before reaching the top of the loose rocks, he stared fixedly. He stopped short. The missionary's tracks, which he had followed, went no farther, but came down again, and it looked as if he had slipped, as if his feet had fled that spot precipitately; Mahigan could see his irregular footprints, like those of a frantic, staggering man, running south across the lake.

Mahigan climbed to the top and looked about. The snow showed that neither human being nor animal had walked upon its surface since he had left it. And yet, the still form was no longer there. Only a pool of blood remained.

"Hunhun! Mati-Manito has carried off my brother to the Land of the Spirits. Now to go and redeem my brother!"

Stoically, he placed his gun upright, with the butt resting on the ground. Kneeling on his right knee, he placed his chin over the barrel, then pressed the trigger with his thumb. All around the prostrate man, the snow was sprinkled with drops of blood and small fragments of brain and bone.

And again, all Nature shuddered as the tragic sound reverberated from hill to hill and died away in the depths of far-off valleys.

7

In his exaltation of mind, Mahigan had lost his shrewdness. Before staggering over the lake, the sliding tracks that descended the loose rocks turned eastward, under the cliff, and stopped near a thick clump of willows. It was on these willows that Mistatim had fallen with the first movement of returning consciousness, for the bullet had merely made a jagged gash in the frontal bone. Father Lozée had heard him fall and, finding him unconscious again and growing cold, had carried him away.

Upon reaching Mistatim's home, he had given him medical aid and baptised his child. Mistatim was soon restored to consciousness. In the middle of the night, the tragic shot had made them all shudder. With one accord, without saying a word, the two men had gone out.

On the flat top of the islet, the pearl-grey radiance of the northern lights shone on three figures under the tranquil sky —a missionary, who stood praying; a motionless form lying on the snow at his feet; and the bowed, kneeling figure of a poor Indian, weeping silently in his heart.

From that night, the Islet of Mati-Manito was known as the Islet of Kitse-Manito. And the Great Spirit, Who is everywhere, Who sees everything, Who knows everything, looked upon His work and saw that it was good.

Mickey Was a Swell Guy

Earle Birney

At first, Joe and me thought it'd take all the summer holidays to save enough from selling Calgary *Heralds* in the morning, and getting subs for the *Pictorial Review* in the afternoon, to buy bikes. And all along we needed bikes to sell the papers. But school wasn't out very long before the headlines got so big, all about Austria and Serbia, that even some guys who got the *Herald* through the mail would buy an early copy on the street too. So, with five bucks Uncle Bill lent me and what I'd made I bought a Bluebird, almost new, for eighteen bucks, and Joe got a CCM, and from them we sold almost as many as Muley and the other big kids who had bikes from the start and regular customers from last year.

If it hadn't been for Mickey, we couldn't of done so swell, though. Mickey had the *Herald* agency and divvied out the papers to the bunch of us on the station platform when the westbound came in. It's a long race every morning up the Station Road and over to Main Street and the hotels, where you can start selling papers to the storekeepers and the tourists. Before we got our bikes, Joe and I woulda had a heck of a time walking up to town, and woulda sold sweet Fanny Adams by the time we got there, but Mickey got around old man Pleming somehow and talked him into letting Joe and me ride up with our papers in the four-horse tallyho he drove for the Hotel Alberta. This was last summer when they still hadn't let motor cars into the Park, and all the Banff hotels used horse buses to run the tourists up from the station.

But we still got uptown late because the hotel buses always have to wait until tourists off the train size them up and decide which one they're going to take. We used to sit on the big black-leather driver's seat beside Old Man Pleming and just ache waiting. The other kids would be pedalling up the Station Road while we were fooling around until the last hayseed or Yankee made up his mind which dump he wanted to sleep in. There weren't no use shoving papers at them because they'd just come from Calgary way themselves and maybe seen the same paper the night before. The thing was to shoot uptown lickety split as soon as the big *Herald* bundles came pitching across the platform from the express car, and Mickey had counted out your share. When there weren't many tourists on the train we were only five minutes behind, though, and sold quite a lot, thanks to Mickey.

Even when we got our bikes, of course, we couldn't pedal as fast as the big kids. They were all about fifteen and Joe and me were only twelve. And Muley was almost eighteen and had wore long pants at school before he quit. He was a year older even than Mickey and weighed 160 pounds. He was a big baloney artist though, and Mickey could lick him easy.

Mickey was sure a swell guy. You know what he did? The first morning Joe and me turned up with our bikes he lined the whole lot of us up before the 8.32 whistled and said that now the *Herald* boys all had bikes they would make a real race of it every morning. So, like in a real race, there would be Handy Gaps and Joe and me would get our papers first. The others would have to give us three minutes' start, except Muley, and he wouldn't get his papers for five minutes. Muley sure didn't like that and started shooting the bull all over the place but there wasn't nothing he could do about it because I guess he remembered how Mickey could clean up on him.

Maybe I ought to tell you about that because it sorta helps to explain how I'm feeling now. Mickey didn't have no kid brothers or no real family, just Old Man Henderson, his step-father, so maybe that was why he was always looking after us smaller kids who hadn't no brothers either, like Joe and me. Muley used to push us kids around a lot. He would pull the corners of his mouth down, and then he would breathe hard and pretend to be mad and start chasing. You never could tell whether he was really mad or not, but you ran like hell anyway because he was a big son of a gun and you darsent take chances.

One day, he started chasing Joe home from school and cornered him in the woods behind the school, and Joe fell trying to hop a brushpile and a stick of willow ran through his cheek. That's where Joe got that crooked scar on his face. The next day, Joe wasn't at school. . . not for three weeks he wasn't. When Mickey heard why, he didn't say nothing until after school. Then he caught Muley in the gravel pit behind Trono's store and first he bawled him out and when Muley started shoving him around he laid into him and give him a real sweet beating up. When Muley tried using his boots, Mickey caught his leg and flopped him hard on the gravel on his back. He weren't hurt too much but he sure was crazy mad. He sat up and grabbed a rock all of a sudden and chunked it at Mickey just as Mickey was stepping over to help him up. It got Mickey spang in the forehead and he went white and his knees caved in and he went down like when Bill Hart shoots some horse-thief or somebody in the movies. He didn't move and his head started bleeding. We was all scared stiff he was dead and Muley beat it for home. But Mickey was just stunned and come to before we could decide what to do.

The next day he had a bandage but he come to school anyway and by golly he caught Muley right after school a second time and was all set to beat the tar out of him again. But Muley wouldn't fight and Mickey let him go after he promised never to use a rock again and not to chase the small kids, and to shake on it. He never did much again, either, not when Mickey

58

was around.

I guess Mickey was the swellest guy in the school all right. He played hockey as good as Dago Hirlick, even better, I always said, and he sure could dive. And he climbed Mount Edith when he was sixteen, without ropes, he and a man from a big mountaineering club in the States. And he could saddle a pack-horse and throw a diamond-hitch like the real packers, and sometimes they would take him out on long trips up to Assiniboine and pay him something too. There wasn't anything Mickey couldn't do. He coulda been smart in school, too, if he'd wanted to. Old Lady Rickman, the teacher, told him once, right out in class, that he ought to study harder and go to college. But that didn't cut no ice with Mickey because Old Man Henderson always took away any dough Mickey made. And he made him work after school, so he didn't pay much attention to kids like Joe and me at school, but he didn't mind you hanging around, not like the other big guys. He would even let you go fishing with him at the Falls sometimes. He always talked to you quiet and honest like, as if you were as big as he was, and he never kidded you. No baloney about Mickey. He had a steady kinda voice and a way of looking at you with his blue eyes real serious. He was the only guy that called me "Matchie" (short for "Matchstick") and made it sound just as good as my real name.

But, I guess I got off the track. I was telling you about how Mickey gave Joe and me three minutes' start pedalling up Main Street and how Muley had to put up with it. The other kids didn't mind much, because, by now there were streamer-heads every day, like AUSTRIANS BOMBARD BELGRADE and GERMANY DECLARES WAR ON RUSSIA. At a cent a *Herald*, even a dumb kid could make a buck in a morning. The only trouble now was to get enough papers, even though the bundles from the express car got so fat they bust open sometimes when they landed on the platform.

Gee Clyde, I'll never forget when the *Heralds* came up with the head: BRITAIN DECLARES WAR ON GERMANY. Everybody knew it already but I sure got a kick seeing that red type shining out when Mickey slit the bundles. First time the *Herald* used red type. It was right across the page. I remember racing Joe up the Station Road with our papers sagging down our wire carriers almost onto the front tire, and the cool air rushing at us, and the sunshine lighting up a snow speck way up on top of Rundle. Even with all the load, I felt like I was soaring and it seemed kinda surprising that my bike was sticking on the road and not leaping right into the air and staying there, the way I felt. We didn't even stop at the Homestead, the first hotel that morning but pedalled all out of breath right into Main Street with Muley just rounding the corner behind us, and the other kids. I was sold out in an hour and made nearly three bucks because there were a lot of tips. People were shouting across the street at each other and some of them were laughing and gosh you felt important—almost like the guys in the poem in the reader about how they brought the good news from Ghent to somewhere, only we didn't have horses. Brownrigg, the butcher, was drunk already and wobbling around outside his store. He was telling everybody he'd been up all night and he wasn't going to bed till they took him in the army. He was going down to Calgary to enlist today, he said, because he didn't want to wait until they opened a recruiting station in Banff. By that time the war would be over, and he wanted to show them a special way to carve up the Kaiser.

Then one day we showed up at the platform and there was no Mickey, and Muley was in charge. He said Mickey had hopped a freight out to Calgary and got a job there. Muley made it tough for us all right, the honyak. There weren't no Handy Gaps any more and he took the extra papers himself and even made us sell him back some of ours at cost after we'd biked them uptown.

We didn't hear nothing about Mickey until almost school-time again. And then, one morning at the station, there he was, but he hadn't come to sell papers. He was in uniform and he sure looked jake. I remember how his buttons were shining bright and he looked clean all over and neat as a woodpecker. He seemed older somehow, and smaller too, but it was Mickey all right, with his big freckled hands poking out of his khaki, and his serious eyes looking out friendly at you.

He said he'd kept quiet about enlisting because he had to lie about his age. But they took him all right after his step-father said he was eighteen when they wrote to him. He'd got in on the First Contingent and was going to England in a few weeks and had got leave to say goodbye. Joe and me felt kinda lost, because Mickey wouldn't be at school next month. But we figured he'd be back in time for selling papers next summer. Mickey said he might even be back by Christmas because the Germans couldn't hold out once the Canadians and Australians and all the rest of the Empire got to France.

When I told my Dad, he was sore and said Mickey was too young and it was only because old skinflint Henderson wanted Mickey's half-pay that Mickey got taken. He said Mickey ought to be kept in Canada as a bugler with the Home Guard. But I was kinda glad Mickey was going right over because, jeez he wasn't the sort of guy that would like sticking around guarding hunkies and being a bugler. He was a real scrapper and they would find out how good he was when he got to the front.

It was sure tough to go back to school in September, with big headlines still coming out. Joe and me got the habit and we would go over to Trono's store at the noon recess and get Jim Trono to show us the headlines, and we'd figure how many papers we coulda sold. After school, I'd bring the afternoon mail home and open up the *Herald* and show Ma the head-lines. When it would be something like SUBS TORPEDO TWO MORE SHIPS; 200 LOST, or CANADIANS SMASH HUNS AT ST. JULIEN: THOUSANDS KILLED, it give you a funny feeling to watch Ma's face. You couldn't ever see anything in Dad's face, but Ma would look tragic-like and sigh, even when it was big victory news, and say something like "When will this terrible slaughter stop?" It was all sort of fun, but you couldn't tell anybody that, and Ma made you feel sort of guilty that you got such a kick out of it.

I remember that St. Julien headline because it was the first big Canadian battle and because, a couple of days after, Mickey's name was in the Cashlety List as Wounded. Course it was kinda worrying and all the kids was talking about it next morning recess. We was pretty sure he musta won a medal anyway and Joe said he bet Mickey killed twenty Huns first. I was sort of hoping he would be sent home to recover and tell us all about it before he went back to the front.

It was May by now, May this year, and the snow was gone half-way up Rundle, and Joe and me were talking already about the holidays and selling papers again. We felt good the war was still on because Joe and me were lots bigger than we were last year and with Muley away—he'd enlisted, too, but hadn't left yet—and only smaller kids going to sell, we knew we would be jake-a-dory even if Mickey wasn't there.

Monday morning, I guess it was a week after Mickey was wounded, I remember feeling Old Lady Rickman was acting queer somehow. During the first lesson, she was frowning a lot though she didn't look to be mad about anything. And she spoke very tired-like so you couldn't hardly hear her, and she didn't seem to care how much whispering we did. She began writing the dates on the board for the history lesson and Mouse McGuire sneaked out his caribou-moss moustache and began pretending to be the Kaiser and rolling his eyes. All of a sudden, she turned around and we thought Mouse was going to catch it. But she didn't look at him; just sat down at her desk and bit her lip. Then she said, and I'll always remember it, she said it so queer and flat-like and very slow:

"Children, word has just come that your schoolmate, Michael Henderson, has died of wounds in the battle of St. Julien. He was shot. In the head."

Then she stopped, and pushed out that sharp jaw of hers, and said something else fast and squeaky that didn't seem to make sense at all:

"It was a very fine head. Much finer than the heads that sent him over there," or something like that.

Then she got up stiff and fast and you could see she was going to bawl and she made a bee line for the door and banged it behind her.

At first, nobody even whispered, and I didn't seem to be able to get my breath, and I was afraid to look at anybody else. And, just when one of the girls began blubbering, in comes the Principal, looking all red and flustered, and said Miss Rickman had been taken ill and we were to have no more classes today and would we go out quietly.

He sure didn't need to tell us to be quiet. You felt almost guilty-like as if you'd been caught doing something you shouldn't, and it was real hard to keep from bawling. I guess it was Old Lady Rickman made us feel queer. I guess she was always a bit nuts. Joe says she was sweet on Mickey, but shucks she was miles too old for him. She was 21, I bet, and besides, Mickey wasn't no girl-chaser. He was a real guy, and I bet she didn't know him as well as we did. We didn't know what she meant about Mickey's head but it made you feel kinda sick. The more I thought about it, the more I got sore at Old Lady Rickman, but Joe said she was looney and didn't know what she was blabbing about. Anyway, I'm glad she ain't coming back next year.

Well, it's July now, and holidays are started. It's swell to go fishing down by the Falls again, and hunting lady-slippers on Tunnel Mountain, and biking out to watch the buffaloes through the Buffalo Park fence, but things ain't the way they were last summer, even though the war's still on. I guess it's because Joe and me ain't selling *Heralds* this summer. We could of, if we wanted, but I got myself a job delivering rush orders on my bike for Brownrigg, the butcher, and Joe decided to try caddying on the links. Of course, we still look at the headlines, sometimes. The Second Canadian Division is getting ready to leave for France now and I guess they really will clean up on the Kaiser this time. But, delivering meat ain't as much a kid's job as selling papers, even if it ain't any better paid.

Sometimes, when I hafta take some meat down to the station agent's, or sometimes, when I see one of the kids selling *Heralds*, or even just when there's a headline about another big victory, I get to thinking of Mickey and what it musta felt like to get hit in the head with a bullet. I wonder if it hurts worse than a stone or whether you just sorta pass out the same way but don't come to again. Gol darn, sometimes I see Mickey as plain as day, his big hands, and his eyes shining out like when he lined us all up to give out the Handy Gaps and I can still see him lying in that gravel pit when Muley conked him, and the blood coming out of his head.

And then the sun don't seem so bright for a while, and the mountains look awful lonely and far off. You feel like you can't tell what's going to happen about anything, and you almost get sore at the war. Because, gosh you'd think a real scrapper as smart and strong as Mickey wouldnta got killed right away, and not even get a VC or DCM or be made a captain after his death or anything, or even kill a lot of Huns first. I sure wish it had been Muley instead of Mickey.

Sometimes I get to feeling so low I even start hoping Muley won't be shot. But, when I said that to Joe, he said I was getting as looney as Old Lady Rickman, and I don't say anything about it to nobody any more.

White Mountains in the Moon

Betty Wilson

There's a ring around the moon tonight, but I can't remember if it's summer, fall or spring. Spring. Meadowlarks were singing when they brought me here.

A ring around the moon. Storm. Wind—? Or blessed rain?

Ring around the moon. Nurse was going to draw the curtain, but I begged, and anyway, the other's sleeping. Choking on herself. I don't mind it here except for that. That and the needles.

The moon's across my bed and I can make the coverlet white mountains in its light. White mountains in the moon! I saw them. Snowfall on the peaks.

They took me to the mountains, Jeannie and the man she married. (What's he called?) It was after Alfie'd—

Mountains in May. Aspens in palest leaf, and mist-blue spruce trees up the slopes. Night. Snowfall in moonlight on the mountain peaks.

Alfie never saw them. Always, he said we'd see the mountains, but—

Is Alfie dead, or did I dream? Alfie. I mustn't call him that. He hates it. Mister. Mister Haythorne. Sand trickled in his grave before the preacher muttered dust to dust.

We crossed an ocean, and almost a continent, he and I before we stopped here on the wind-burned plains.

He said we'd see the mountains. But he never did. Merely half a day by car. He made the Rockies seem as far away as the cliffs of Cornwall's coast, but they're only half a day by car.

There's a ring around the moon tonight. Rain? Rain on the sand to make the wheat grow tall. Oh, we had harvests. 1915, the first year, and 1927, the year that Mister bought the truck. But he never understood machines. When it broke down he couldn't fix it. Someone told me, laughing, that he almost gave the thing away.

Perhaps this year there'll be a harvest, but I don't know how I'll plant the field. Horses are hard to catch, and the harness tangles of straps and buckles. Can I remember how it goes? Sweat-pad and collar. Hames and hame-straps, britching and belly-band. But the lines—I don't remember. Mister will— What am I thinking of? Mister's gone. I don't know where the horses are.

I wonder if the ducks came back? Alfie says the slough wastes two acres of our land that should grow grain. But I like the ducks and the frogs that sing there in the spring.

And what grain have we grown except for twice? Others. Parkers, Thomases. Even Pedersens, and they scarcely spoke a word of English for the first five years I knew them. Tractors and combines and—

If Mister understood machines— Who uses horses any more? But who am I to talk? The cream separator baffles me.

Am I talking to myself again? I must not do that. People will think me strange. The Thomas boy laughed at me. Forgot that he was in the house. I looked out to see our cows in Parker's grain and scolded Mister because he hadn't fixed the fence. Mister wasn't there.

There's a ring around the moon tonight. There was a ring around the moon the night before—

I hate the wind!

Mister'd been away all day and all the day before. Gone to buy seed grain and stopped for a quick one with the chaps.

I milked the cow and fed the calf and baby pigs. And waited.

Such a cloud! Green as rotten chicken guts.

Mister didn't come, but the cloud came up the sky. Supper. Salt pork boiled three times before I could choke it down. Never touched salt pork again.

The cloud like death, green death, rising, and rising overhead, until I was swallowed in lightning and wind, and the twisting cloud that ripped and dipped and tore the land. Deafening silence. Couldn't breathe. Then— Could a house be snatched up like that and flung against the earth?

The stove pinned me against the wall. A mercy that the fire'd gone out. After the rain, silence, and a burrowing owl calling and calling in the dark.

At first light Mister came, and others with him.

Mrs. Thomas took me home. Told me time and again that I'd been fortunate.

"Not even badly hurt! And there's little Mrs. Lakey dead, and two motherless children. And what's a man to do with motherless children? *We've* all got more than our share."

All but me. So when they had the house set up and patched enough to live in, I took the children. But never *my* children. Perhaps at six and eight it's too much to expect.

The father disappeared. Just walked away. We never heard of him again.

At school, the other children laughed at clothes I'd made the girls. Jeannie complained about our food, and it was poor. Others had roast beef and pie.

Before the Christmas concert, when she was ten, Laura asked me not to smile so much. My old false teeth were chipped. Gums like dirty brick.

We bought a Christmas tree that year. I can't remember how we managed it. Mister took walnuts and cut them into baskets with a hack saw. Cut his fingers doing it, and cursed, but they were fairy things, those baskets. I hung them on the tree with coloured darning yarn.

Pedersens had glass baubles on their tree.

As they grew older, the girls begged time to spend with

neighbours, so, between their visiting and school— It was dull for them at home. No games. Only my old tales, and the radio when we could afford to have the battery charged.

Jeannie was a pretty thing. I never said it, but I think I looked like that when I was young.

We'd never had a party in our house, but for her fourteenth birthday—

Mister went to town that morning, early. Things to be bought. Candles for the cake, lemons for lemonade, and Jeannie's present from the post office; the Eaton's parcel with a dress. He met some chaps. The party with no lemonade, no candles, and no dress had been over hours before he came.

The girls grasped him, each by an arm, and twirled him round and round, singing Here's Mister Haythorne now until his legs gave way. He thought it was a game.

Soon after that the boys began to come around. Jeannie married a fellow she met when she was hired girl at Thomases'. Rancher's son from the Cyprus Hills. I wish I could remember what he's called.

Laura? I wish I knew. Left at sixteen. There were letters at first. Said she was slinging hash in Regina. Slinging hash— I don't know what that means. How long ago? It must be years and years.

And so, we're alone again, Mister and I. The work gets harder year by year. When fences need fixing Mister sits beside the stove, and there's a broken window in the kitchen with cardboard nailed across the pane. And the floor— Lumpy knots in old boards. The table rocks because of them.

At hog-killing when Mr. Parker and Mr. Thomas helped— I tried to square the table before I called them in to dinner, but still it rocked. It shamed me to see them laughing secretly at slopped-over tea.

It must have been last spring that Alfie drove the team to town to fetch some flour. The horse stood, unfed, unblanketed in a chilly wind. Takes strong arms and a steady head to manage horses, cold and hungry. And he'd been with the chaps.

They said he'd landed head-first on a rock when the horses ran away. Children on their way to school found him, and the team and broken wagon tangled in the corner of a fence.

Sand trickled in his grave before the preacher muttered dust to dust.

Jeannie and her man took some days off spring work, and that's the time I saw the mountains in the moon.

Jeannie's husband asked me if I needed anything.

I told him that I had a bit put by. I did. $30 in a coffee can. I said I'd rent the farm to neighbours for a share of crop. Plenty to keep an old woman whose wants are few.

And so they went away, content.

People said the farm was overgrown with weeds, worn out, and wind-eroded. Nobody wanted it.

There was a cow, and the garden. But the cow crawled under Parker's fence and cut herself. After that she was no good for milk. Frost killed the garden in September. I saved potatoes, beets and cabbages, but they don't last forever.

Pedersens found me asleep. Wrapped me in blankets, picked me up and brought me here. The snow had gone and meadowlarks were singing.

The doctor's young enough to be my grandson. He says I have cornflower eyes. Cornflower eyes in leather, old and brown and wrinkled as my father's Sunday boots.

The nurses try to feed me, but I choke. And the needles hurt.

White-topped mountain— Gone. The moon has climbed the sky. If I move my head I still can see—a little of the ring.

Magpie

Helen J. Rosta

"She died there," his father said, "a young girl like that all alone in the city." In the steaming kitchen his parents seemed to be huddled together and the fact of death which at first had been clear and pronounceable took on the significance of their whispers and occasional glances at him. He strained to catch words, snatches of meaning.

"Danny," his mother said. "Run out and gather the eggs."

"I already did."

Sharply. "Well gather them again."

"Hurry up," his father said. "Do what you're told."

Danny retained one vivid memory of the Nash girl at the big picnic on the river shortly before she had run away to Vancouver. She had been wearing an old black bathing suit splattered with moth holes and when she jumped up and down in the water her white skin seemed to glimmer like stars. She laughed a lot and splashed water into the faces of the young men who lounged at the river's edge smoking cigarettes and talking earnestly among themselves. The men, blushing, pelted her with sand until old Mrs. Nash, red-faced and puffing, heaved herself above the mass of sprawling bodies and told the girl to behave and not make a spectacle of herself.

"What's a spectacle?" Jim Morrison had asked Danny.

"Something people look at, I guess."

"Were they looking at her?"

"I dunno."

"Stupid," Bill Davies sneered, "they were looking through them holes in her bathing suit."

The chicken house was dim, filled with the chalky smell of chicken droppings. Danny felt around in the straw for the imaginary eggs. Only one grey, speckled hen sat like a spectre on the nest. He reached under her, his hand sinking into the soft, warm feathers. He could feel her heart beating rapidly. The hen made soft, guttural sounds in her throat and pecked gently at his hand as he drew the still moist egg from under her.

He walked slowly back to the house. The late afternoon sun sent thin yellow rays across the yard. Around the doorway the climbing gourds hung in strands, the frozen leaves shrivelled into black umbrellas. When he opened the door, Danny heard his father's voice, "the body back for burial."

"Oh dear," his mother sounded distressed, "I suppose we'll have to go to the funeral."

"I suppose. . . ."

His mother saw him then, standing just inside the door. "Little pitchers," she warned.

During supper they ate silently, doggedly, as if they were waiting for him to excuse himself so they could continue talking. It seemed to Danny that the conversation hovered unheard over the supper table and that if he reached up he could pull it, word by word, into consciousness.

What was this mystery, Danny wondered, this mystery that was stranger than death? Death was being stiff and cold and silent. This other thing, this mystery that hung in the air was strange and secret.

That evening after he had finished his chores, he lingered in the kitchen, casually sipping a glass of water. His mother, bent over her ironing, did not look up. Finally he said, "She wasn't old." Up to now death had been associated with old spidery men and women.

"Who wasn't old?"

71

"The Nash girl."

His mother pushed the iron into an apron tuck and held the garment up for inspection before speaking. "No, she wasn't old. She was scarcely more than a child." Standing close, Danny smelled the hot brown odour of the ironing. His mother smoothed a pillow slip with her hand and slid the iron over it. She seemed to be talking to herself, "You bring them into the world and you do the best you can but you never know. . . ." Danny waited but he sensed that she was not going to continue. He tried again.

"I guess they didn't want to bury her in a big city and everything. I guess that's why they're bringing her back." He had never been to Vancouver; it was far away; across mountains which were sometimes so high that trains had to snake back and forth through tunnels to get over them.

He wondered if a train was on its way now, bringing the Nash girl. It must cost a lot of money, he thought, to bring her back and everyone knew that the Nash family was awfully poor.

"A mother wants to be near her child. . .and she'll be with the rest of the family. . . they're all in Fairfield cemetery, the old folks and the girl's Aunt Susan on her mother's side, and the little boy they lost. . . they'll be able to keep the grave up. It's not like leaving it to strangers."

Fairfield, Danny thought, it was a long way from the railroad station. He wondered how they would get her out. He imagined skinny Mr. Nash in his dirty overalls driving the pick-up into town, Mrs. Nash red and perspiring beside him.

"Will they bring her out in the truck?"

His mother looked shocked. Her face was pink and there were beads of sweat on her upper lip. "Of course not. There's a special car—a hearse, a big black car with curtains at the window and they put the casket in the back. . . . Now listen young man, get on with you. Can't you see I'm busy? I want to finish this ironing sometime tonight and besides, you haven't done your homework."

"I don't have any."

"Do it anyway."

Danny followed the fenceline on his way to school. The grass was stiff with frost and crunched under his feet. By the time he reached the road his canvas shoes were damp and cold. Deep ruts, gouged in the road during the last rain, were frozen now and he could feel their sharp edges through the thin soles of his shoes. The road led to town. Danny wondered how long it would take him to get there if he just kept walking, walking past the school, past the bell, past Miss Adams looking out of the window. . . .

The kids were gathered on the steps of the school house, excited, the big ones talking, the youngest hanging on the fringes of the group, straining their ears.

"My brother took her to the movies once. . ."

"Hey, what'd he. . . ?"

"Daddy said she was no better than she should be. . . ."

"No better than she should be?"

"Never mind, you're just a little kid. You wouldn't understand."

"My brother said. . . Look I'll tell you after. . . I don't want to talk in front of the babies. They might run home and ask their mothers what it means. . . ."

Danny did his arithmetic and listened in while the teacher worked with the other students.

Miss Adams wore pretty dresses and she smelled so nice that whenever she bent over his desk he thought of a field of clover. His mother said Miss Adams had a face like a valentine but his father said her legs were like stovepipes. Now, when he looked up she was standing in front of his row, frowning at him. "Danny." He hurriedly took out his reader.

"All things bright and beautiful," Miss Adams read. Danny fingered the grimy page of his book. "Now class," Miss Adams said, "I want you to make your very own list of things that you

73

think are bright and beautiful."

Danny bent over his scribbler. Were people ever beautiful, that is, beautiful to look at, like a dog or a horse? His mother said that even if people didn't look beautiful, they could have an inner beauty, a beautiful spirit. But when the spirit was gone, even an ugly spirit, the person was dead. He thought of old Star who had been struck by lightning, just a little burnt spot in his mane but there he was in the morning, stretched out on the hill, his legs rigid as poles, his mouth open. Motionless, even when the flies settled on his eyeballs, motionless, stiff. . . the Nash girl jumping up and down in the river. . . but with her there was something else. . . .

"Danny," Miss Adams said, "Get to work."

He wrote "horses" on his page. When the sun was high, old Star began to swell and they hooked a chain around his neck and dragged him off into the middle of the field and set fire to him. The smoke was black and smelled of kerosene and burning hair. . . .

"Danny," Miss Adams scolded, "Danny, stop daydreaming and get to work."

At recess they flocked under the poplar trees bordering the school grounds to watch Bill and Ray set a snare. Bill climbed a tree and twisted the silver-grey wire around a branch. He skewered a jam sandwich to a twig slightly above the snare. The wire was invisible against the grey bark.

When Bill jumped out of the tree he landed against Danny, knocking him down. "Hey Stupid," he snarled. "Can't you even get out of a guy's way?" He jabbed Jim Morrison in the ribs, "Hey Jim, what do ya think sa matter with Danny boy? He's been acting dum-dum all morning and now he doesn't have enough brains to get out of a guy's way when he's jumping out of a tree for Christ's sake." Bill grinned savagely. His teeth were covered with yellow fur. "Maybe Dannyboy is going crazy."

"Ya," Ray interjected. "He must be goin' crazy. . . actin' just like Bug-eyes." Bug-eyes, who was lingering in the shadows, looked up warily. In the thin fall light his face was as pallid as the belly of a frog. A glimmer of fear showed in his pale prominent eyes.

Jim Morrison began the chant:

Bug-eyes. Bug-eyes. Who buys your groceries?
We do. We do. Cause you're on Welfare.
Bug-eyes. Bug-eyes. Go away and eat the flies.

Bug-eyes began to sidle away. For a moment Danny thought that he had been forgotten and felt relieved, and at the same time a little ashamed. He was sorry for Bug-eyes who cried a lot and smelled of urine but he didn't dare let on. He pretended he didn't see when the big boys made Bug-eyes eat the dead flies that collected on the window sills.

The group took up the chant. Bug-eyes retreated farther and the boys made a movement as if to rush after him but suddenly Bill swung toward Danny. His big teeth glittered. "Hey fellows," he cried, "maybe Danny boy wants to eat flies. Maybe that'll perk him up."

Danny recoiled. A wave of nausea hit him but he forced himself to remain outwardly nonchalant. They were fanning out, forming a circle around him, the big boys hanging back a little, smiling. At any moment they might attack, pinning him down, shoving flies between his teeth. He glanced around for a weapon. A clod lay at his feet. He bent and grasped it, hurling it straight ahead. It hit the tree by Jim Morrison's head. Chunks of dirt flew in all directions and one of them struck Jim Morrison in the eye. He began to howl.

"Bug-eye yourself," Danny yelled. The big boys laughed.

"If you blinded me, I'll tell my dad on you," Jim Morrison whimpered.

"Tattle-tale," Danny sneered.

"Sissy," Bill said. "Sissy." The bell rang. They ran toward

the school crying, "Sissy, Sissy, Sissy."

During class Danny covertly watched Jim Morrison to see if he had indeed blinded him. Jim kept his hand over his right eye but when he stood up to read he forgot about it and Danny was vastly relieved to see that the eye was still there and that Jim wasn't blind.

At noon the sun broke through the shallow overcast. The leaves on the poplar trees were the colour of butter. "It's nice enough to eat outside," Miss Adams said. They jostled one another for coats and lunch buckets.

"You come too, Teacher," the girls said.

"Girls!" Bill whispered contemptuously. When the teacher ate with them they felt constrained to stay together. Otherwise the boys ate apart.

Today they crowded on the south side of the coal shed. They pressed against the walls to escape the sharp autumn wind that cut briskly through the feeble heat that reflected from the building. Their lunch pails smelled of tin, home-made bread and ripe tomatoes. Bill and Ray, rendered shy by the forced intimacy of lunching with the teacher, gobbled their food. They nudged one another impatiently. "Come on, we gotta go look at our snare."

Danny heard their shouts from the poplar bluff, "Magpie. Magpie." Whooping in triumph, they brought it flopping around the corner of the shed, its legs still entangled in the snare which the boys were now handling as a line, flicking the wire and driving the bird ahead of them. The magpie floundered, wings outstretched, white feathers speckled with blood. Its legs, mangled in the wire, spilled delicate string-like tendons out of the skin.

From time to time the bird made a lunge as if to fly but succeeded only in pulling the snare tighter. Inspired by the magpie's efforts to get off the ground, Bill shouted, "Hey look. I've got a kite." He flung the bird into the air. The magpie, anticipating freedom, flapped its wings in wild spurts. The

76

boys fed out the wire and the bird soared, straining away from them. A sudden jerk and it plunged to the ground where it lay heaving, beak agape, its tiny pointed tongue lifted, soundless.

Danny looked to Miss Adams. Why doesn't she do something? Why doesn't she do something? Stop them. He couldn't read her face. She stood close to Bill and Ray, almost between them. She did not move. He dropped his head, ashamed to look, staring down at his dirty canvas shoes where Miss Adams' shadow stopped. Stopped, he noticed with surprise, right at his feet while Bill's and Ray's shadows shot on by like two dark giants. Bill's shadow arm moved rhythmically as if he were throwing a ball into the air. One of the girls began to cry.

"That's enough boys," Miss Adams said. "That's enough now. I think you had better kill it." Bill's arm moved convulsively, as if he could not give up the game. "Please Bill," Miss Adams said. She looked vulnerable, diminished.

The magpie's eyes were rimmed with blood. Danny grabbed a stick and hit the bird on the head, striking again and again. He heard Bug-eyes screaming, "It's all right to kill magpies ain't it Teacher? 'Cause magpies are bad birds." The beak opened wide as if in protest, the tongue subsided, the magpie's body jerked for a moment and then lay still.

Danny first heard the roar of the engine and then he saw the hearse. It came down the road, a great black limousine, moving slowly as if the jolting on the violently rutted surface might dislodge its cargo. The children wheeled away from the magpie's carcass.

"Look at the crazy car," Jim Morrison yelled. "The crazy car's got curtains."

He doesn't know what it is, Danny thought. They don't know what it is. Jim Morrison began to yelp. Shaking his head from side to side, he galloped toward the car. Screaming, the others charged after him, heedless of Miss Adams' shrill, "Children. Children." Danny too, exhilarated by the puffs of dust and the smell of exhaust, ran blindly after the car, rushing toward the stiff cold body of the dead girl, dull now, not gleaming with river water, while Miss Adams' voice rose in a crescendo. "Children. Children. Come back. A disgrace." He imagined her stumbling after them in her silly high heels, helpless, imploring, and he began to grab rocks from the roadside and hurl them after the car until it had disappeared from sight.

The Harvester

Robert Kroetsch

He came in shortly after six o'clock that morning, in a cattle truck off Highway 13. Maggie was just opening the roadside café for the day's business and was alone, and she came from the kitchen when the door slammed and went to the counter as two men sat down.

The trucker pushed his cap back with a greasy hand and flicked the menu from between a ketchup bottle and a napkin holder. "Ham and eggs scrambled—in a hurry," he said. "Black coffee."

Maggie nodded and turned to the old man. She saw his quiet grey eyes devouring yesterday's cakes and pies, stale behind the counter. She pretended not to see as he opened his hand on a few coins like a poker player looking at his cards. He closed his hand again, then paused before he said, "Coffee with a little cream. . . and buttered toast."

Maggie hurried to prepare and serve the orders, and after that she hoisted her heavy body onto the boss's stool behind the cash register and listened while the trucker gulped his food and complained about the road. She watched the old man.

He was a harvester, apparently, and he drank his coffee slowly, not talking, and when the trucker slapped some change on the counter and went to the men's room, Maggie stood up to pick up the change. "You better get a wiggle on, mister," she said, "or you'll miss your ride."

"I'm staying," the harvester said.

Maggie started to question him, but she heard the coffee boiling over in the kitchen and she hurried away. She did not return till the trucker yelled so-long, and then she came out to say so-long and went to the front window to watch.

After the truck was gone she stood staring for a moment; she stared across the highway at the flat fields, glinting yellow in the cold morning sun, at the wheat lying swathed and ready for the combine. Then she turned away with a jerk, knowing that work would take the dull sleepy ache out of her bones, and she began to pick up the dirty dishes.

She left the harvester's empty cup sitting in front of him. "Working around here?" she asked.

"Come west to work every year," the harvester said.

"A combine man?" Maggie asked.

"I'm a field pitcher."

Maggie stopped with the dishes stacked on her arm. "You mean, you were a field pitcher. You used to be. But you ain't since they shut down the threshing machines."

"I'm a field pitcher," the harvester replied.

Maggie shrugged and took the dishes into the kitchen and came back with a damp cloth. She was wiping the counter when suddenly the harvester asked, "You a widow woman?"

"Twice married and twice widowed," Maggie said. "No family either time." Then she noticed the harvester's quiet steady gaze on her rings, and she felt obliged to explain. "I didn't take up short-order cooking till my second husband died with his heart. He was a body-repair man. My first husband owned the biggest steam-threshing outfit in these parts."

The harvester smiled for the first time. "Fun working then," he said.

"Fun cooking then," Maggie said. "You cooked meals, not pig feed. And you fed men. But you got to change with the times."

It was a saying she had, and usually people said, "Yeah, you got to." But the harvester only dropped two coins on the

80

counter. "Eating and everything," he said. "It was fun then."

Maggie stopped dead. Toast and coffee wasn't a pleasure for this man. It was as if someone had switched on a light in a shadowed recess of her memory. She stopped suddenly and forgot the hamburger she'd neglected to take out of the freezer the night before, and she was a young woman again, just come to her brother's homestead from Ontario. She remembered the young men coming west at harvest time; the trainloads of young men, laughing, shouting, singing, fighting over a pretty girl, pitching bundles all day and dancing half the night. She remembered now: city boys with blistered hands, their jaws set hard beneath their smiles, country men from the eastern valleys, staring in disbelief at the broad plains. She remembered sixteen strong men at a plank table, threshers eating like threshers and praising the cook by the way they glanced at a steaming dish; one man eating enough for three and topping it off with a wedge of her famous Dutch apple pie. And she saw, in her mind's eye, a hundred lean, bronzed, handsome harvesters, licking their pie plates clean and glancing up with sheepish grins and asking for more.

And suddenly, standing there with a dirty dishcloth in her hand, remembering—suddenly she saw this one bent, lonely, ill-fed survivor, this one old harvester from all that migrant crowd of young men. And she stared at his gnarled brown hands shaped to fit a pitchfork handle; empty hands that once lifted a grain-heavy bundle or a washtub full of lunch or a laughing girl. She saw the old brown suit coat, too big over the new bib overalls and the checkered cotton shirt. She stared and forgot about cold cereals and club sandwiches and cake mix. And she pushed back the nickel and dime and signalled the old harvester to follow her into the kitchen.

When the waitress came to work she fluttered in at the kitchen door like an injured bird and pleaded, "Please, Maggie. You know what the boss said."

"Shhh," Maggie said.

"You know," the little waitress insisted. "You know what he'll do if he catches us feeding somebody free."

Maggie raised a stained square finger to her lips. "See?" she said, and with a slight nod indicated the old harvester bent over the kitchen table.

The little waitress only frowned her disapproval.

Maggie dropped her hands into her apron pockets and pointed again by staring intently at the harvester's boots, hooked around the legs of the backless chair. "See?" she repeated.

The harvester's boots were as new and shiny as the neckties in a country store. Their black toe caps were not stubble-worn. The new bib overalls were not frayed at the cuffs.

The waitress now saw, saw the absence of wear and understood, and nodded with pity and reluctance.

"Just keep the boss out of the kitchen till after breakfast," Maggie said. She handed the waitress an empty tray and turned again to her task.

She would fill an order for ham and eggs or hot cakes, and then she would turn to the old harvester and serve him another helping of riced potatoes and dumplings and gravy and another slice of roast beef. "Just like it used to be, old timer," she would say. "Holler if you want more."

Usually he nodded and leaned away from his plate to let her dish up more creamed carrots or buttered peas or corn on the cob. But one time he said, "No hurry at dinnertime, Ma'am. We got to wait for the horses to eat."

It was then Maggie realized he wasn't quite all there any more.

He was eating heartily and didn't notice when Annie Melnyk, the waitress, complained, and Maggie thought he didn't notice later when Annie stuck her head through the window-like opening that joined the kitchen to the café. "Where are those sausages, Maggie? The customer's in a hurry and the boss just got here and he'll be asking about them in a minute."

"Be ready in a jiffy," Maggie said.

Annie sniffed and looked around and saw the pie sitting on the windowledge to cool; saw the criss-crosses of flaky crust and the rich cinnamon colour and the sweet, mouth-watering promise of sliced apples in creamy sauce. "Maggie, we'll get our walking papers if the boss sees that. He told you never to make Dutch apple pie because pie mix is cheaper, and he'll know you didn't make it to sell."

"Keep him glued to his cash register," Maggie said, and she slid a plate of sausages through the window to Annie. "We can't quit at this stage of the game."

The old harvester raised up and looked around the table. "Ma'am."

"Maggie Winters," Maggie said.

"Mrs. Winters," the harvester said. "I'm afraid I'm causing you a lot of trouble. I'd better leave."

"There's no hurry. We'll let you know whenever there's a ride out of town."

"I'm getting a job here," he said. "I'll pay you as soon as I get a job."

"Forget it," Maggie said. She slapped a slice of pressed ham into a pan. "Don't worry about it."

The old harvester pulled a cheap pocket watch from the pocket on the front of his bib overalls. "It's nearly nine," he said. "The farmers'll be in any minute now, looking for help. Will that little girl tell them I'm here?"

Maggie flipped the ham over. "She'll tell them. Don't worry." She moved over to the sink to wash some of the pans she had used to prepare the big dinner.

The harvester looked around to see that his things were not in the way. When he came into the kitchen he took off his coat and hung it on a nail, and then he carefully laid his faded cap on the floor beneath it and placed his new kangaroo tan leather gloves in the cap. He rolled up his shirtsleeves and the sleeves

83

of his woollen underwear, and he turned his shirt collar under, and Maggie was confused for a moment, for she had forgotten. Then she remembered and hurriedly cleared the sink, and the harvester washed, scrubbing his neck and ears as if he had been in dust and chaff, blowing vigorously as he lifted the cold water to his face with both hands and rubbed, and he ran his wet hands back over his heavy grey hair when he finished. And after he dried, using Maggie's towel, he went to his suit coat for a comb and slicked his hair down meticulously.

By that time Maggie had the table set and a bowl of noodle soup waiting, and she changed her apron when he wasn't looking, and brushed at her own grey hair. And she remembered how she always put on a clean and freshly starched dress before the threshers came in.

Now the harvester pushed himself back from the table and fished inside the bib of his overalls to a shirt pocket for his papers and tobacco.

"Just a minute," Maggie said. "Your dessert will be ready in a minute." She wanted to stall him while the pie cooled, and she asked, "Have you been through this country before?"

"I had a 32-day run here. That's why I came back."

"That was quite a few years ago," Maggie said.

"Only 24 years. 24 years this fall. 32 days without a breakdown or a stop for the weather. But it was snowing the afternoon we finished. The bundle teams raced in from out in the field with the pitchforks bouncing on the empty racks and the men shouting to each other. And by the time they got unhooked the ground was white. It sort of made you want to sing."

Maggie nodded.

"The farmer was a man from Bruce County and he had a keg of beer and some cheese and crackers and dill pickles and home-made sausage waiting, and we went to work and cleaned that all up. And then we went into town." The harvester rubbed his knuckles. "A crew from the next town was in the beer parlour, and we started mentioning how much wheat we could thresh in a day, and we took a dislike to the way they suggested our figures might not be exact. So we up and threw them out of the place. We had a Swede from up near Camrose who could pick up a man in each hand. He must have been seven feet—"

"That was 25 years ago," Maggie said. "My first husband was still alive. We got threshed that fall, but our neighbours didn't, and Ben helped them, digging the stooks out of the snow. They threshed one morning when it was 27 below."

"I slept in a straw-pile bottom on a night when it was just about that cold," the harvester said. "That was my second year west. But it got warm when it started to snow, and in the morning my boots were clean out of sight. We threshed all that day out of a stack and spent half the next night on the open prairie, moving the outfit eighteen miles."

"I was cooking for a steam outfit my second year out here," Maggie said. She wiped her hands on her apron and leaned against an old meat block. "Used to take a team and democrat and drive into town for groceries once a week. I remember one time a cowboy followed me on his saddle horse for three hours, trying to make a date for a dance over at the MacFarlanes' house. He was carrying a real six-shooter." She smiled. "But if my crew had seen him they'd have skinned him al—"

"Hey, Maggie!"

It was Annie Melnyk's voice at the little window. "Quick! Where's that order of fried eggs?"

"Lordie me. I forgot!" Maggie said. She heaved her heavy body up off the meat block and with a sigh picked up two eggs in one hand and cracked one on the edge of a frying pan. "Help yourself to the pie," she told the harvester.

While Maggie waited for the eggs to fry she remembered other harvesters; young men who made a stake and didn't come back, or better still, young men who came and stayed. They home-steaded, waiting for spring, enduring the long winter in tar-paper shacks set on the bald prairie. They watched the nail heads whiten with frost and watching, remembered with hidden tears the joys of the past. They dreamed with a bursting eagerness the great lonely dream of the future; turned the grey sod black in their dreams, loved beautiful women, built gracious homes. And through the long dark nights they huddled in thin blankets and listened to the wind.

And they were old and prosperous now; men who had jabbed their fork tines into the dry earth and squatted on a stook and passed around a jug of water; weary men who had tugged a package of makings from a sweaty shirt pocket; men who had known the comradely warmth of "Care to roll one?" And they blew lazy clouds of expensive smoke now, and wintered in front of television sets, and paid cold cash for their wives' fur coats.

But here was one old man, still wandering, still sitting up all night in a day coach, watching the yellow fields appear in the dawn. Still drifting back and forth, stubborn and stupid, Maggie thought. And she, just as stubborn and just as stupid, and too old to boot, was risking her own and the waitress's job, just to give him one square meal. Just to feed one old harvester who wasn't quite right in the head anymore. He had caught her at a soft moment and now she regretted it, and she turned on him, roughly. "Just what do you do in the wintertime?"

"The bush," he said. "I get a job in the bush just north of Lake Superior."

I might have guessed it, Maggie thought: the prairie and the forest. One old man living like the sole surviving member of a tribe, wandering onto the prairie in the summer, back into the shelter of the forest in winter. "You got to change with the time," she told him. "What's a field pitcher nowadays?"

The old man straightened up and turned with a polite and indestructible pride. "A good field pitcher can make a threshing crew," he said. "He ain't just the man who helps the teamsters load the bundle wagons."

"I didn't say that," Maggie said.

"Give me a 28-inch machine and six greenhorns and six new teams, and by the end of a week they'll be a threshing outfit."

"I'm not arguing," Maggie said. But she was losing her temper at his blind perseverance. "I'm not arguing about that."

"Give me six dudes," the old man said, "and by the end of a week they'll know how to build a load of bundles that won't slide out and will still be easy to pitch into the feeder. They'll know how to lift a fork all day without breaking their backs, and they'll just wear gloves in the morning while it's cold, and they'll have calluses instead of blisters."

"Sure," Maggie said. Her anger was a lump in her chest now. "That's just fine. That's great. But you got to change. My boss doesn't break his back doing anything and he doesn't wear gloves except at funerals and he doesn't get any handouts from anybody—and his calluses are all on his behind."

The harvester looked away and his voice dropped almost to a whisper. "Give me a new teamster and a team just in off the range, which is all you can find nowadays, and where will you find a man to train them? I've taught grown men how to tie the reins to the rack and how to turn by touching a pitchfork to the reins. These new men don't know what gee and haw mean, let alone the horses know. And when I get finished, a team won't always be trying to eat a stook, and it won't run away if some partridges fly up, and it won't be scared of the tractor."

Maggie slid the fried eggs and an order of toast out to Annie. "I understand," she said. She was ashamed of herself, but her anger was still a tight dry knot. "A good team is just dandy. Except they got combines now—self-propelled. They do the work. They work day and night when the weather's fine. And when it rains you don't have men and horses standing around idle."

The harvester looked up at the ceiling and paused before he answered. "I imagine it don't rain too often in here."

"Eat your pie," Maggie said.

"Those rainy days were good ones," the harvester said, "even if they didn't make much money. We'd lay in the bunk shack all day and listen to it hissing where it ran down the stovepipe. And I'd play "Prairie Redwing" or something on the mouth organ and you'd hear feet keeping time or somebody humming maybe, and after everybody was slept out there'd be a game of rummy and maybe some sock mending to do, and there'd be good talk about other places and riding the rails and the good times we'd had."

"And you'd eat too much and sleep some more," Maggie said.

"If we had a good cook. And sometimes we'd hit a poor one, and we'd work like the devil to get off the place, and one hour before suppertime some evening a good cook would get word that she was getting the threshers."

"That happened to me more than once," Maggie said. But this time she was only soft for a moment. "Now I could give them a short-order hamburger."

"Maggie!"

It was the waitress.

"What now?"

"That hamburger. Did you forget it?"

"Hold your horses. It was half-frozen."

"It's for the boss."

"Lordie me," Maggie said. She pressed down on the grease-spitting hamburger with a spatula. "We're done for."

"There's a trucker outside," Annie said. "In a yellow oil truck. He's going up the line aways."

"Quick," Maggie said, turning to the harvester. She picked up his cap and gloves and took his coat off the nail. "Go out the back door and around to the front, and a man in a yellow

88

oil truck is waiting for you."

"Is there any threshing up the way he's going?"

"There'll be something or other. Quick."

The harvester stood up and started putting on his coat. "Excuse me Ma'am, but could I take a piece of that pie with me?"

"Sure, anything," Maggie said. She pulled the waxed paper off a loaf of bread and turned to cut the pie. The harvester had eaten half.

"Hurry," Annie said. "The boss is coming."

The harvester slid the wedge of pie into his suit-coat pocket and went to the back door. But in the doorway he stopped.

Maggie raised her hand as if to shoo him along, but he would not be interrupted, and he thanked her quietly and politely. Maggie stopped pushing as he talked, and he only stepped away as the boss elbowed Annie aside and stuck his head in at the serving window.

"Where the hell's that hamburger?"

Maggie turned from the open door and saw the pinched sallow face in the little window, like a frame, and she did not say a word. She went to the stove and flipped the half-done patty of meat out of the pan, onto an open bun. She slapped it onto a plate and dumped raw onions and relish and mustard onto and around it. She tilted a ketchup bottle upside down and hit the bottom with the palm of her hand, and ketchup spattered the hamburger and the boss's hand.

"Watch out, that stuff costs money. Don't waste—"

Maggie spun the plate across the counter toward the window.

The boss caught it in self-defence and started to shout. But his eyes grew puzzled and he picked up the hamburger and pushed it woodenly into his gaping mouth, and he retreated from the little window.

Annie Melnyk, frightened and astounded, burst in at the kitchen door. "What's the matter?" she whispered. "What's—"

Maggie's face was as radiant as a child's. Her set mouth was

89

smiling softly and her eyes were bright and two tears clung to the cheeks of her tired, careworn, sweaty, red face. "He remembered," Maggie said. She caught her rough stained hands together in front of her apron like a woman recalling a lover. "After 25 years, he still remembered. He called me Mrs. Rinehart."

"You're Mrs. Winters," Annie said. "Don't you feel—"

"Rinehart," Maggie said. "My first husband's name. After 25 years he still remembered Mrs. Rinehart. He remembered my Dutch apple pie!"

Annie shrugged and noticed the pan sizzling empty on the stove and moved it, and outside a truck roared and was gone.

And then, in the quiet morning air, there was only the distant drone of the combines.

Patterns

W. O. Mitchell

Often on a Saturday night, when he found himself badly blocked in a sermon, Mr. Cameron found release in tying dry flies; it was a solitary and mesmerizing occupation which somehow freed his mind and imagination. The loose feathers lifted and slid over the desk top under his gentle breath; the completed flies increased one by one, resting high and light on their hackle tips at his elbow. With each fly the tension loosened more and he experienced a little of the satiety that attended the netting of a trout itself. Rings slowly widened and spread to grassy banks; sunlight disked and danced on green water; clear bubbles and foam were borne slowly circling; mosquitoes whined thin; grasshoppers leaped clicketing; and he had broken off for himself a warm and humming fragment of August.

Plato, he felt, would have approved of dry-fly tying; the feather filaments were so spirit-light they could lift and float the heavy dross of the material hook, ideal camouflage raying from the barbed and lethal matter. These were classical flies to ride bravely down summer streams, drifting like waterborne stars on their tantalizing course over slicks and riffles where hungry rainbow lay.

The minister leaned back in his chair and poured himself another cup of tea. Somehow tonight the fly tying did not soothe—certainly not enough to rid his mind of the thought of a Rory Napoleon missing for three days. And why was it that he must always be so concerned for the Napoleons? He was too practical a man to imagine he could bring them spiritual nourishment. They were not members of his congregation, though that would have been impertinent if they had been in actual want. To his knowledge they never were; they were warm; they were fed; they were clothed; their goats and their 80 weed-infested acres and Rory's job as town garbage collector seemed to take care of their material needs. Their health was the continuing concern of Dr. Fotheringham, who made sure they got to the clinic once a month.

The minister could understand the doctor's interest in the Napoleons; he could also appreciate Mr. Oliver's concern. The police magistrate was the tidiest man in town; proprietor of the Oliver Trading Company General Store, law was only an avocation with him but it was his first love, all the same. In the impeccability of the lawn about his house, store window displays, grocery shelves and counters, one could see that order was Mr. Oliver's passion. His interest, the minister felt, might simply be an attraction to an opposite. Mr. Cameron could not so simply explain his own fascination, a disturbing one dating from the time that he had first come to his charge in Shelby ten years ago. Deliberately then he had set out to discover all he could about the Napoleons; Dr. Fotheringham had been a most fertile source of information.

In Rory Napoleon's veins, the doctor thought, flowed the blood of Brittany tinted with some Basque and mingling with one-quarter Piegan contributed by his maternal grandfather, Chief Baseball, who had signed the Blackfoot Crossing Treaty in 1878. These had been given Rory by the French half-breed mother, who had met and loved under lodge-pole pines a remittance cowhand in 1908, so that Rory as well boasted the proud blood of the line MacCrimmon, composers of pibroch and pipers to the chiefs of Scotland. Mame, his common-law wife, was ten years younger than Rory; like Ontario cheddar she was pure Canadian. Their offspring: Buster, Byron, Avalon, Evelyn, Ester, Elvira—living—and Violet, Herbert, Calvin and Clarence, who had died at birth or in infancy, carried the Breton-Basque-Piegan-Scot-Canadian blood.

Town legend had it that Byron had been born on Dominion Day and on top of a ferris wheel at the thirty-ninth Annual Shelby Fair, Light Horse Show and Rodeo. This was not precisely true, Henry Fotheringham had explained to the minister.

"Byron was born exactly nine months after Dominion Day," the doctor said. " 'I always been fussy about the ferris wheel,' Mame told me. 'Fair was almost over an' I told Rory I'd like one more ride before we went home. Ferris wheel broke down. We never did get a good type of ferris wheel at our fairs you know. An' there was Rory an' me with the motor broke down an' our seats swingin' from the top of midnight for a good hour. What else was there for us to...' "

A slight, dark and insouciant man with a rather wild eye, Rory could be seen daily in the Post Office just before mail time. He wore a faded blue jacket, its breast pockets lined with a battery of fountain pens and pencils. Usually he took up a position, leaning against the wall near the door and under the WANTED posters and the civil service examination notices. He had no mail box so that when Mr. Fry lifted the frosted window and swung in the brass grill, Rory took his place in line with those lesser individuals whose mail came in a lump under the initial letter of their surnames in General Delivery.

Mr. Fry at the Post Office handed him out regularly: the Shelby *Chinook*, both the Calgary dailies, the Regina *Leader-Post*, the Winnipeg *Tribune*, Nor-west *Prairie Farm Review*, the *Country Gentleman*, *Maclean's*, *Star Weekly*, *Saturday Evening Post*, and Dr. Wine-singer's Calendar Almanac. "I see by the papers today," was Rory's unfailing gangplank to conversation. He was unable to read or write.

With their herd of 47 goats the Napoleons lived just at the edge of town and next to the farm of Dan Sibbald. Year after year of goat trespass had thinned Mr. Sibbald's patience until an afternoon in the Maple Leaf Beer Parlour just three months before, when Rory had laid open Dan's head with a beer bottle. Mr. Cameron had talked it over with Mr. Oliver, the police magistrate, before he visited the Napoleons.

He found only Mame at home, accepted her invitation to a cup of tea, and came directly to the reason for his visit. "Mrs. Napoleon, I've called to see you about Rory."

"Uh-huh."

"And about Dan Sibbald."

"Did you?" There was little warmth in the red-rimmed eyes.

"Something has to be done, Mrs. Napoleon."

She turned away, took down a brown teapot from the wooden board that formed a shelf above the stove. As she began to shake tea into it she said, "What?"

"I've talked it over with Mr. Oliver. . . ."

"Him!"

"And he's had a talk with Dan Sibbald. . . ."

"Might have known Oliver'd get into it with his big flat English feet. . . ."

"Mr. Oliver has been very just about. . ."

"Always had it in for the Napoleons—can't leave us alone!"

"Mr. Oliver! Oh, I don't think so. . . ."

"Well, I do."

"But why would he have it in for. . ."

"I don't know why," Mrs. Napoleon said, "but he always has—always will—stubborn—he was to drownd they'd find his body upstream!"

"But Mr. Oliver is willing to give Rory a chance. That doesn't sound as though he. . ."

"What kind of a chance?"

"He is willing to use his influence with Dan Sibbald—persuade him not to press charges against Rory either for trespass or for assault."

"Is that right?" Some of the coldness had vanished from Mrs. Napoleon's eyes. "Don't sound like Oliver."

"But it is."

"Don't sound like Dan Sibbald either," she said. "What's Rory got to do—apologize to Dan?"

"That would help, Mrs. Napoleon—to begin with."

"What else has he got to. . ."

"It's not Rory who has to do something else—it's you."

"Me? How?"

"I'd like you to have Rory interdicted—for his own good—for your own—for the children. . . ."

"An' if I don't put Rory on the Indian List?"

"Then Mr. Oliver will have to let the law take its course."

"That sounds more like Oliver."

"There'll be a summons tomorrow."

"An' Rory'll have to go up before Oliver."

"Yes."

She tipped the boiling kettle over the teapot.

"I'm sorry, Mrs. Napoleon," Mr. Cameron said.

She set a cup before him. "I believe you."

"I wanted to talk it over with Mr. Napoleon but Mr. Oliver said it wouldn't be a good. . ."

"He's right. Wouldn't have a chance if Rory got tipped off first." She sat down in the backless wooden chair by the table. "If it's gotta be done—I'm the one's gotta do it."

"Will you do it for us?"

"I won't do it for Oliver."

"Will you do it for Rory?"

She shook her head. "Kids has it bad enough without Rory goin' down to Lethbridge for a couple months. I'll do it for them. Drink your tea while it's hot. And I'll do it for you."

Now, in his study, Mr. Cameron set aside his empty teacup, stared at the half-tied grey hackle held in the slant nose of the fly-tying vise. It had been so much easier than he had anticipated it would be—and persistently successful; to his knowledge and to Magistrate Oliver's. Rory had put in a sober three months; the goats had stayed in their pen on Napoleon land. Pangs of conscience had come more and more infrequently to

95

the minister as he assured himself that the man's loss of drinking privileges had benefited his work for the town, his wife, his children. Of course there had never been any questioning the desirability of the end; it was the means that had disturbed Mr. Cameron. He would have felt so much better if he had talked it over with Rory first, given the man a chance to agree. It just wasn't right to push people about—even for their own good, for in a way then it stopped being their own good, nor was it such a satisfactory good. There was a comparable difference between a rainbow taken on bait and a rainbow taken fairly on a dry fly.

Obviously with the man missing for three days, it hadn't worked out so well after all. For three months he had deluded himself. Behind the drily casual façade the Napoleons presented to the world, the minister had always sensed a faint threat, but exactly what was threatened or to whom, he had never been sure. He knew only that the threat was there—vaguely ominous—persistent. Somehow—tonight—the minister told himself as he leaned forward over the fly vise—the Napoleon threat was the strongest it had ever been; in the heart of some dark place a hidden Rory waited—had always been waiting—but now was almost through waiting.

For three months Rory Napoleon had waited; for three months his tongue had stuck to the roof of his mouth and his throat had got stiff for the tickle of beer and the earth taste of beer. But Cameron and Oliver and the law had said God Save the Queen to it and that was all there was to it—he couldn't do a thing about it. Couldn't go in the place even. Well, send the law victorious—didn't know beer was glorious! Beer never hurt him—never hurt anybody. Let everyone suck beer down and not a drop for him!

At the end of three months he had called on Artie Buller, black-mailed the taxi man into selling him five jugs of wine improved by the addition of grain alcohol to the mother catawba. Artie had resisted making the sale until Rory had

threatened to inform Mr. Oliver that Artie had many customers among Napoleon relatives still resident on Paradise
Valley Indian Reserve. Rory left Art's Taxi building with his
five jugs of Artie's Own; among his cousins out at Paradise
Reserve it was more familiarly known as Old Wolverine.

There was one thing to be said about being interdicted for
over three months, Rory Napoleon decided: when a man did
get hold of the stuff it had gained in muzzle velocity, increased
its range, and improved penetration power. He had quite soon
achieved a holiday state of total anaesthesia, reclining on sweet
clover hay in a corner of the pole shed south of the goat pen.
Three days and four and one half jugs later he awoke chilled,
in dusk musty with the smell of mould, aslant with dust-
vibrant bars of late-afternoon sunlight.

He teetered out of the shed and across the yard to the goat
pen. He made a place for himself by pushing aside the brush
that Byron had piled on top to keep the goats from leaping to
freedom and Dan Sibbald's land, then climbed up and hooked
his heels on a lower pole. He stared down upon the 47 goats
below. It might have been a matter only of common clues in
eye and jaw and nostril; Rory was not interested in the per-
ceptual why; he only knew that now he looked down upon
citizens of Shelby, members of Shelby Rotary, the Activarians,
Knights of the Loyal Order of Homesteaders, the town council,
North Siders.

"You—Mrs. Fotherin'ham," he addressed the white nanny
just beneath him, "can go spit up a rope, for I ain't emptyin'
another can for you. I'm human same as anybody else, ain't I?
Don't that mean somethin', Oliver?" He was speaking to the
billy behind Mrs. Fotheringham, a one-horned ram with a
glassy wall eye fixed upon him. "Don't it mean somethin' if a
person's a human? Ain't it more important to be a human than
to be a horse or a dog or a goat? It's a head start, Oliver!"

But Mr. Oliver had turned and was making his slow way
through the herd to the opposite side of the pen. Rory was sud-

97

denly filled with uncontrollable anger against Mr. Oliver—
all of them. He half rose from his perch.

"I was born human!" he shouted after Mr. Oliver. "I'll die
human! I eat human! I drink human! I am human! I'm me!
I'm Rory Napoleon!"

All the assembly had turned their attention up to him, but
they were just goats now. 47 plain goats. "I am a human," he
explained carefully to them. "What's more I am the only human on this whole earth, which is Rory Napoleon."

He grabbed the butt end of willow brush by his thigh and
wrenched it loose from the pile; he attacked the rest furiously,
flushed with wine, elation and exertion. It was only a moment
till he had the top of the pen cleared of the brush that had been
piled there to keep the goats inside.

"All right—all right now!" he yelled at them, "you can
come up outa there—nothin' to stop you now! High-yuh!" he
shrilled as they huddled together at the far side of the pen,
blinking up at him in the astonishing sunlight.

"Get your lazy nose out of it, you shag-anappi-spring-heeled,
china-eyed English bastard, Oliver! Hough-hough-hah-hup-
yaah, Mrs. Tregillis an' Revrund Cameron! Hell's about to go
out for recess!"

In 30 seconds the goat eruction was complete.

Rory Napoleon had selected a Saturday night precisely right
for the outrage that followed his release of the goats. It was the
Saturday night of the month on which the Shelby and Greater
Shelby Emergency and Disaster Relief and Civil Defence Committee met. It was as well the night that the Cameo Theatre
was exhibiting to its only packed house since the advent of
television to Shelby, a vista-vision religious spectacular show-
ing the slaughter of 5000 Christian extras and 9000 animals
in the Coliseum as well as the crucifixion and the sack of
Rome. The Russians had just shocked the world with the an-
nouncement of another successful satellite; ten days ago a 200-
yard section of the Trans-Canada Pipeline had exploded 29

98

miles east of Shelby; Northern Lights the night before had tented the entire sky with frightening brilliance. The day, the week, the month, the year were unique in a chain of chance fragile with coincidence which might have parted at any line short of the final anarchy.

As soon as Rory Napoleon had herded his 47 goats to the head of a brightly lighted and teeming Main Street, the Saturday night traffic came to a halt and quickly bottled the street back in both directions to the ends of the block. The goats left the street itself and took to the sidewalk, trotting as far as Oliver's Trading Company General Store, where Mayor Frazer (goat) caught sight of the fresh vegetable display and led a splinter group of seven through the open door. Eleven others followed Mr. Oliver (goat) to the front of the Maple Leaf Beer Parlour, where one of the outgoing patrons obligingly held open the door. To any of the Napoleon goats a doorway was a familiar phenomenon and now in their frightened bewilderment they automatically sought the security of a confinement they'd known for three months.

Nettie Fotheringham (goat) took her diminished retinue of 28 as far as the Cameo Theatre where the double doors stood wide for the changing of show. They entered the darkened interior just as Alaric's Visigothic hordes breached the outer gates of Rome. Mr. Cameron (goat), a dissenter from Mr. Oliver's (goat) Maple Leaf Beer Parlour group, trotted to the corner, went up a side street and out of the business section entirely. Three blocks away he came to the shelter of a vague cluster of buildings and stopped to clip the dry grass there.

Within the Maple Leaf Beer Parlour the banter and laughter and friendly argument had changed to curses, grunts, shouts and roars as beer-inflamed men and sober goats mixed together in bleating, butting, kicking, struggling nihilism over a floor awash with spilled beverage, broken glass and chairs and overturned tables. The concussion of the fray vibrated the common wall the beer parlour shared with Totecole's Hardware next door, and Morton Totecole, looking after the store during his father's coffee break, took down the double-barrel ten gauge from the shotgun rack and slipped in two number-four magnum shells.

Torches had been touched to the Palatine Hill; gladiator and Goth battled against the leaping technicolour flames; Cameo Theatre patrons in outside seats were aware of numerous rustling, moving shapes tapping along the darkened aisle.

Unable to dislodge Mayor Frazer (goat) and his grazing council from the fresh vegetable and fruit counter, Mr. Oliver (human) admitted failure and phoned Millie Clocker, asking her breathlessly to ring for the police and as well have Fire Chief Alsop turn out a couple of available men. In his excitement he did not explain to Millie that there was no fire and that the men were needed for extraordinary duties. Millie set off the fire siren first and then plugged in for the Mounted Police.

Mr. Cameron (goat) had been grazing, minding his own business, when the fire siren on the fire hall beside him set up its scooping wail. He catapulted to the roof, picked his way along the ridge, at the end of which he could discern a towering skeletal structure; his hooves clanged as he soared upward and came to brief rest before climbing to the top, high over the town buildings.

On hearing the fire siren Cross-cut Jack Brown (Rescue and First Aid), Malleable Jack Brown (Flat-Bottom Boats and Flood Control), Pipe-fitting Jack Brown (Shelter and Alarm) went to the Main Street window of the Ranchman's Club smoking-room where they were holding their meeting of the Shelby and Greater Shelby Emergency and Disaster Relief and Civil Defence Committee. They saw the Mounted Police cruiser wheel around the Royal Bank corner with red light flashing, sensed the confusion in the street below, and heard the rioting uproar from the Maple Leaf Beer Parlour. Pipe-fitting Jack Brown ran to the phone and gave Millie Clocker the blue alert.

She signalled the red, however, which would sound the siren again, ring St. Aiden's Church bell, warn the hospital staff, summon Dr. Fotheringham with stretcher bearers, and flush out Ollie Pringle—with ambulance and Pulmotor.

Morton Totecole stood before the Maple Leaf Beer Parlour with the loaded ten gauge in his hands; he had no intention of using it as he had seen sheriffs and their deputies do on CBC; he was simply waiting to hand it to someone older and much braver than he. The fury within the Maple Leaf had abated, for Taffy had gathered his waiters and some of the patrons at the bar end of the parlour, formed them into a slowly advancing line of men facing a slowly retreating line of goats. Taffy himself stood to one side of the door, ready to throw it open at the strategic moment that the goats were close enough to recognize the triangular gestalt of themselves/the door/freedom.

On the street before the Maple Leaf, Morton Totecole heard the sounds of two new sirens; the one on the fire engine racing south on First Street, the other on Ollie Pringle's ambulance racing north on First Street. St. Aiden's bell began to tongue the night. The fire siren gave three preparatory whoops before it took up the sustained ululation of the red alert.

The church bell penetrated the stirring darkness of the Cameo Theatre where skinned barbarians were garrotting fine old Senators with their own togas and carrying shrieking Roman matrons through falling marble columns and burning rubble. The scrambling in the aisles and the elastic hysteria of three sirens instantly convinced all patrons that the theatre was ablaze.

It was as though the downtown section of Shelby had become the toy of some idiot giant child and was now activated by a great hopper trickling alarm that filled each heart with a cargo of dread till it ran downhill, was tripped, spilled, only to be refilled again, this time with grains of consternation, the next with fright, then terror, and finally panic. As Cameo patrons erupted from the theatre they thought was burning, the herd burst out of the Maple Leaf. Ollie Pringle's ambulance reached Main and First Street at the same moment as the fire engine. Morton Totecole went down in a smother of goats. Mr. Cameron (goat) put out a moist and inquisitive nose to the thing of gleaming glass and metal cable before him. Morton's hand convulsed on the triggers of the ten-gauge goose gun, discharged both barrels at a distance of eighteen inches from the 26-foot plate window of his father's store. The shotgun blast coincided with the superb head-on collision of the ambulance and fire engine as well as with the crackling detonation that signalled the electrocution of Mr. Cameron (goat), who had grounded the power plant transformer with a Queen's Birthday fountain of sparks and a sheet of violet light that winked up the town and the district as far as the correction line. Citizens of Khartoum heard the explosion; those of Tiger Lily said they had.

In the pitch darkness of Main Street there were too many people and too many goats. Humans stamped blindly toward the Royal Bank corner and were brought up against the barricade formed by the fire engine and the ambulance. They swept back through the lightless night, driving the goats before them. Some sought safety in cars, others in stores. Those in cars and trucks turned on their headlights so that a grotesque magic-lantern show of goats and humans was projected against the flat faces of the stores; it was neither vista-vision nor technicolour, but the sack of Rome had been pale by comparison.

Within the stores kerosene and mantle lamps, flashlights and candles were brought out, but they had hardly been lit before full light came on from the town's auxiliary power plant. Some order was reasserting itself, for many now knew that there had been no fire, invasion, earthquake, pipeline explosion, falling Russian satellite—just the Napoleon goats. Except for Maple Leaf cuts and bruises now being treated by Dr. Fotheringham there had miraculously been no serious injuries.

Right after he had turned the goats into the top of Main Street, Rory Napoleon had gone back through Hepner's lumber yards, retraced his steps over the CNR bridge, made straight for home and the feed shed. There he fell upon the hay, reached down for the last of his jugs of wine. He finished it.

Slightly after midnight Constables Dove and Clarkson entered the shed. One took Rory by the legs, the other by the armpits. They carried him out, a snoring hammock, between them to the cruiser, headed for the town and the barracks.

The Reverend Cameron finished whipping the head of the last grey hackle, touched it with a bead of black enamel, released it from the vise and laid it down by the others. He had intended going to bed by eleven, but with the power break which had put out the lights, it had taken him till now to tie the dozen flies he liked to complete at one sitting. He leaned back in his chair and as he sighed, three flies drifted over the varnished surface of the desk. Fly patterns—Plato's patterns—God's patterns—man's patterns—oh, so terribly fragile! Always the Napoleons to destroy them; that was the Napoleon threat indeed.

Mirror, Alberta

Stephen Scobie

"The house was already ablaze when we got to it."

I reached over and switched on my tape recorder. The story-teller looked at me and asked, "What did you do that for?"

"This time," I said, "I want an accurate record of one of your stories."

Charlie objected. "All that will give you is the words," he said, "not the story-teller's presence, the warmth of this room, the precise moments at which the listeners shift in their chairs, the beam of headlights sweeping the ceiling..."

"The words will be enough for now," I said.

The story-teller agreed. "The words are always enough."

"Go on with your story," I said.

"What story?" asked Harry.

"The story as it happens; the story as it begins. It has begun; you are in it now."

"I missed the beginning."

"The house was already ablaze when we got to it."

"What house?"

"You see?" The story-teller turned to me. "There is the proof of all I have told you about narrative. I give him one sentence, and already he is curious. I can elaborate the whole story out of that one sentence, and his responses to it. What house? he asks. And after that: Why was it burning? And then: Who are 'we'? How many? Male or female? What are the sexual relationships between us?"

"I'm not interested in the sexual relationships," Harry insisted. "It was only the house I asked about."

"Confine yourself to the house," Charlie suggested. "No sex."

"Hey!" I objected. "Whose story is this?"

"A good point," the story-teller conceded. "The ownership of a story is always in doubt. Can I really say it is mine? Sometimes it seems as if I discover the story, already there, and all I do is to give it to other people. So if it neither begins nor ends with me, in what sense is it really mine?"

"Get back to the house," said Harry.

"I hope it's not in Quebec," said Charlie. "I'm tired of stories about burning houses in Quebec."

"Shut up and let him tell his story."

The story-teller smiled. "The house," he began, "was not in Quebec. It was in Mirror, Alberta."

"Where?"

"A small village in central Alberta. It is called Mirror. I was born there."

We looked at him doubtfully. None of us knew where he had really been born, but none of us believed it was in a village called Mirror, Alberta. But then, it is a fallacy to equate the "I" of any story with its author.

"You may not believe there is such a place," he went on, "but there is. It is a very small place. Its largest building is a two-storey wooden hotel. It is close to a minor highway, not far from Bashaw. It exists."

"How did it get that name?" asked Charlie suspiciously.

The story-teller took on a pedantic air. "It is alleged," he said, "that the name was chosen by the Grand Trunk Civic Development Company, which at the time placed a good deal of its advertising with a London newspaper called the Daily Mirror. I must admit, however, that I never saw a copy of this periodical in Mirror, Alberta."

"It's possible," Charlie conceded. "People choose names for

the craziest reasons."

The story-teller made a concession in return. "I admit, the name would be a tempting one to invent, simply for symbolic effect. Shakespeare said that narrative must 'hold the mirror up to Nature.' Perhaps what I am doing is holding nature up to Mirror."

Charlie pondered this. "That doesn't mean anything," he decided.

"Quite right," the story-teller admitted. "Never take anything on trust, especially abstract generalizations. Trust the tale, not the teller, as David used to tell me. Oh well. But there is a place called Mirror, and I was born there, and that is where the story takes place."

"Were you really born there?" Harry asked.

"If I wasn't," the story-teller replied, "then perhaps my mirror-image was." That served Harry right. It had been a stupid question.

"There was a school in Mirror, Alberta," the story-teller went on, "presided over by a severe Scotch lady."

"Scots," I corrected automatically.

"Scots. She had come from Edinburgh 50 years before, carrying with her two precious things." He paused for effect. "Two precious things," he repeated. Nobody asked him what they were, so he told us.

"The first was a book: a book of Latin grammar. It was called, I recollect, *Rudiments of the Latin Tongue*, and it had been written by a man called Thomas Ruddiman. We used to think it funny, of course, that a man called Ruddiman should have written a book called Rudiments. 'Ruddiman's ruddy Rudiments,' we called it. Childish wordplay, but instructive. There was one very impressive thing about this book."

Again he paused, and this time used a drink of beer as an excuse. "What was that?" I prompted at last.

"It was published in 1714," he said, "and Miss Henderson possessed a first edition. I imagine it was very valuable. It had been in her family, she used to tell us, for many generations. Let me put your minds at rest. It was not destroyed in the fire."

"What fire?" asked Harry.

"The house was already ablaze when we got to it."

"Oh that fire."

"We began with a fire and we shall end with a fire. But now we are in the middle. Now we are at the second precious thing."

"A photograph," suggested Charlie.

The story-teller nodded.

"A photograph of a young man she was going to marry."

The story-teller nodded.

"He had come out before her to break a quarter section of land near Mirror, Alberta."

The story-teller nodded.

"But shortly before she arrived, he was killed in an unfortunate accident, so she became an embittered spinster schoolteacher, imposing the rudiments of Latin upon the children of Mirror, Alberta."

The story-teller nodded.

Charlie snorted. "I thought so. What a bunch of clichés. Can't you make up a better story than that?"

"Ah, but I did not make it up. You did."

"You nodded."

"Perhaps. But that was only to signify that what you were suggesting was a possible line of development. Personally, I had something quite different in mind for the second precious thing."

"What was that?" I asked.

"No, no, it doesn't matter," said the story-teller. "Let us adopt Charlie's version by all means. It will serve quite adequately."

"If it isn't true," said Charlie sarcastically, "at least it's a mirror-image of the truth."

"But of course it's true," protested the story-teller. "In a story, everything is true once you say it is. His name was James McColl. He came from Fraserburgh. He was 28 years old when he died, five feet eleven inches, 180 pounds—and sturdily built, none of it was fat. He had blond hair, blue eyes, and, so my father once told me, a gorgeous bass voice."

"Sang psalms in the church choir," I suggested.

"Exactly. But he's not important, because, as I told you, this was all 50 years before. When I knew her, she was old and small and tough and scary. I know my Latin to this day. *Quot sunt partes orationes?*"

"What's that mean?"

"How many parts of speech are there? It was the first sentence in the grammar book. The answer is *octo*."

"You mean the book itself was in Latin?"

"Ruddiman's was. And that's how she taught us. Spoke to us in Latin, about Latin. Total immersion. The best method."

"I never could learn languages," said Harry. "My boss keeps threatening to send me to the branch in Montreal."

The story-teller absorbed this in his stride. "Miss Henderson had never been to Montreal. Or even to Edmonton. It was rumoured she had once gone to Red Deer."

"Why would she want to go to Red Deer?" I asked. It was the opening he had been working for.

"To see a lawyer, I believe. Mostly she didn't trust lawyers, because they couldn't read her writing."

Charlie laughed. "Some of my clients have terrible writing," he said. He's a lawyer.

"Miss Henderson's writing was exquisite," said the story-teller. "It was an old-fashioned copperplate, written with a real quill pen. A thing of beauty. She had been taught it when she was a very young girl, by an old uncle who worked in the Advocates' Library in Edinburgh. Will you permit a digression?"

"I thought," said Charlie, "that we'd already gone through at least three digressions."

"Not at all. We've been very logical. And it's a short digression." The story-teller took another drink. "The uncle explains where the *Rudiments* came from. But Miss Henderson, so far as I know, never made the connection. Thomas Ruddiman, you see, was the first curator of the Advocates' Library, practically its founder. And if she had an uncle who worked there. . ."

"You mean," suggested Harry, "that this valuable first edition might have been stolen?"

"Oh no, I shouldn't think so. You need the utmost moral probity to work in the Advocates' Library."

"Nowadays," I offered pedantically, "it's the National Library of Scotland."

"Indeed," said the story-teller, unruffled. "I didn't know that. And neither did Miss Henderson, I'm sure. She never mentioned any connection between her treasure and this uncle— the one who taught her copperplate handwriting. He told her, you see. . ."

"Have we finished the digression?" Charlie interrupted.

"I believe so."

"Good."

"He told her, you see, that it was lawyer's handwriting. So she absolutely distrusted anyone who was a lawyer and couldn't read her writing."

"But surely," I objected, "her handwriting can't have been so difficult to read that nobody in a Red Deer lawyer's office could make it out."

"Probably not," agreed the story-teller. "Except for one little thing. She always wrote it backwards."

"Backwards?"

The story-teller smiled. "Mirror writing," he said.

We looked at each other and groaned. "Did you have to do that?" we asked him.

"It's not a joke," he insisted. "She really did. Beautiful, elegant spirals—but completely illegible, unless you held it up to a mirror. I think she did it quite unconsciously most of the time. Most of the time."

He paused. Affronted by our groans, he was making us work for this one. "Most of the time," I prompted. But he wasn't going to give in so easily. "Most of the time," he repeated.

"When wasn't she unconscious about it?" I asked laboriously.

"When she was conscious about it."

I breathed deeply. "And when was that?"

"When she taught it to me."

"You mean you can do this mirrored copperplate handwriting?" asked Charlie.

"Of course," said the story-teller smugly.

"Prove it." Charlie sounded as if he were snapping a trap shut on a coyote. He whipped out a piece of paper and a ballpoint pen.

"A goose quill would be better," the story-teller ventured.

"Chicken!" accused Charlie triumphantly.

"Goose," said the story-teller mildly. He picked up the pen, and wrote something on the paper with a great flourish. We all gathered round to look at it. It was all beautiful, elegant spirals—but completely illegible, until we took it into the bathroom and held it up to the mirror. The handwriting was very beautiful. It read:

"The house was already ablaze when we got to it."

"I was coming to that," said the story-teller.

"Wait a minute," said Harry. "The house can wait. What I want to know is, why did this Miss Harrison—"

"Henderson."

"—why did this Miss Harrison teach *you* mirror writing?"

"I was her favourite pupil."

"Why?"

"That's a long story," said the story-teller.

"Cut it short," said Charlie.

"Okay," agreed the story-teller. "To cut a long story short, it was all about encyclopedias."

"Here we go," said Charlie.

I had heard this one before, so I took the opportunity to change my tape. It's the story about the farmer's wife and the encyclopedia salesman, and how the farmer gets mad and chases the salesman around the yard with a shotgun, and how the family is left with only volume one of the encyclopedia, and how the young hero reads that one volume from cover to cover and is an absolute expert on everything that begins with the letter A but anything from Babylon on has him stumped. I had heard it before, so I got my tape changed and was just starting it up again by the time the story-teller had arrived at:

"Aeneas. I knew everything there was to know about Aeneas. So when we got round to *arma virumque cano* I was all set."

"That's the first line of Virgil's *Aeneid*," I explained. I too had a classical education, though not from Ruddiman.

"And after class that day Miss Henderson took me aside and told me to come round to her house Saturday morning."

"But when you got to her house," said Harry, "it was already ablaze."

"No, no, no, no, NO," said the story-teller. "That was later, and I wasn't alone. And besides, it wasn't her house at all."

"But you said it was," Charlie objected.

"I never did," said the story-teller, and my tape proves he was right.

"So you went round to her place on Saturday morning," I prompted.

"Certainly not," he replied. "It was ploughing season. My dad wouldn't let me out of the fields till after sundown, and by that time I was so tired I just fell asleep on my way upstairs to bed. No, I had to play hooky from church the next morning to get to learn mirror writing. Miss Henderson never went to church. She was an atheist."

"Fairly unusual," I observed, "for a schoolteacher in Mirror, Alberta."

"Nobody dared mention it," the story-teller expounded confidently. "Some say it was all due to the shock she got when poor Tom McColl died."

"James McColl," Charlie corrected.

"Did I say James? That was his brother. Not that it matters, they were both killed together the same dark winter's night. Drowned in a slough within sight of the church. That must have been what turned Miss Henderson against religion."

"Maybe she worshipped the old Roman gods," I suggested.

"Entirely possible." The story-teller swept up this suggestion too. "Saw herself as a kind of Vestal Virgin, so rumour had it, and poured libations of home-brewed liquor onto her dining-room floorboards. They were always in bad repair. The local carpenter once told me. . ."

"Can we please get back to the burning house?" said Harry. "I have to go home soon."

"Well," said the story-teller, "I'm just about to run into a little difficulty here. One of you gentlemen specified no sex in this story. And I'm not sure that I can get this story over the next hurdle without a little sex."

"Panting, he ripped the flimsy covering away from her globular bosom." The others gave me strange looks.

"All right," said Charlie. "A little sex. The minimum necessary."

"I'll do what I can. I had just got round to mentioning the local carpenter. . ."

"Is *that* necessary?" asked Charlie.

"His daughter," explained the story-teller patiently. "His daughter."

"Oh, that's all right then."

"I should think so too. His daughter's name was Aurora. Will you permit a short rhapsodic interlude concerning her beauty?"

"No."

"Very well, we'll take her beauty for granted. She was eighteen years old, and I was fourteen, and I was head over heels in love with her. From a distance, you understand. But—and here I will exercise a remarkable restraint and economy—we contrived to become sweethearts."

"I'd like to hear how you managed *that*," said Harry.

"Another time. Today we have the minimum necessary sex. Another time I will recount to you the misadventure at the Church Social, the episode in the hayloft, the assignation by the elevator, the saga of the splintered sideboard—an epic romance to delight the populace and spread my name in lights. Another time, Harry, if you don't mind."

Harry received this offer ambivalently.

"We had become sweethearts." The story-teller's voice dropped an octave; he glanced around to make sure his audience was spellbound. "Not lovers, you understand—this was Mirror, Alberta—but sweethearts. And I wrote her long, passionate love letters. . ."

"In mirror handwriting," his spellbound audience chimed in unison.

"Exactly." His voice thrilled. "And she—Aurora—would go to read them in her secret retreat, out in the garden, a small wooden summerhouse. . ."

"A *summer*house?" asked Harry.

"Well, actually, more of an outhouse," admitted the story-teller.

"Get my coat too when you're out there, will you Charlie?" Harry was getting to his feet.

"One day," the story-teller continued undaunted, "one very hot day she went out there, with my entire collection of love letters. My entire collection. And sitting there reading it, she was roused to the heights of physical passion. . ."

"A minimum," said Charlie, handing Harry his coat.

"I was resting," the story-teller said expansively, "on top of a haystack, when she came to me. She climbed the haystack as light as a zephyr and as hot as a chinook. For the sake of your delicate sensibility, Charlie, I'll pass over what happened next. But meanwhile back at the outhouse. . ."

"Good night, Stephen."

"Good night, Charlie. Good night, Harry."

"Good night."

"She'd left the mirror, which she used to read my letters, propped on the seat; and the sun's rays, coming through the outhouse door, reflected off the mirror directly onto the pile of my love letters. . . . Have they both gone, Stephen?"

"Indeed they have."

He smiled. "Good. Now I can tell you the *real* story. Why don't you get a couple of beers and put another tape on your machine?"

I did so.

The story-teller leaned back in his chair, closed his eyes, took a swig of his beer. "The words are always enough," he said at last. "The story as it happens; the story as it begins. It has begun; you are in it now. It is always the same story, over and over. The only problem is to know where to begin. So where shall I begin?"

"The house was already ablaze when we got to it."

An Anonymous Letter

Henry Kreisel

A sudden commotion woke the boy. He sat up in bed and listened half-asleep to the raised voices of his mother and father. They were quarrelling. The boy tried to make out their words, but he couldn't, and so he got up and groped his way out of the dark bedroom, and when he opened the door and stood in the hall their voices seemed shriller and uglier than before. His parents had often quarrelled, but their quarrels had never been so violent before. As he came closer to the living-room, he felt his heart beating and he was afraid.

His parents stopped shouting at each other as soon as they saw him, and a brooding, dangerous silence seemed to settle over the room and was almost worse than the tangible voices. The strong light in the room hurt the boy's eyes and he closed them for a moment and everything was red and yellow. He rubbed his eyes with his fingers, feeling wide awake and yet sleepy. That was a curious feeling.

"David!" he heard his father say. "Why did you get up?"

The boy opened his eyes, and became suddenly aware that his father was fully dressed. He had his glasses on, and he wore a dark-grey, striped suit and a red tie, and his hair was neatly combed. So he couldn't have been in bed yet, the boy thought. He must have just come in a little while ago. It must be very late. Was that why they were quarrelling so violently?

"I woke up because of the noise you and Mom made," said the boy quietly.

He moved his eyes slowly away from his father and looked now closely at his mother. She was standing there in her dressing-gown. In her hand she held a large, crumpled piece of yellow paper. Her hair was dishevelled. Loose locks seemed to be sticking out all over, like pieces of thick string. Her face looked very pale without any rouge or lipstick. She looked pretty awful, the boy thought, gazing down at the floor. Not like the glamorous women in the movies. They were always sleek and beautiful, with their hair curling and their lips fresh, even when they'd just got out of bed. He knew deep down that people never really looked so lovely when they got out of bed, he knew he looked pretty awful in his wrinkled-up pyjamas, with his hair all mussed. But his mother could look pretty nice sometimes, when her hair was all set and combed and her face made up, and when she wore a sleek-fitting dress and high-heeled shoes and nylon stockings. But now she didn't look very nice, and he wished he didn't have to look at her.

"What happened?" he asked. "Why are you shouting at each other?"

"Because your mother believes everything, just so long as it's written down," said his father.

"Ask your father where he was until nearly three in the morning."

"I told you," said his father calmly. "I was playing poker over at Eddie's place. It got late. That's all there is to it."

"Was *she* there, too?" asked his mother. Her hand closed tightly around the piece of yellow paper, and the boy saw that she was trembling.

"Rubbish!" his father cried. His face was red, and blue veins began to show on his temples, but he was trying to control the rising anger, and said with elaborate irony, "Sure, sure. There was Eddie, and Arnold Griffin and Joe Holmes and—and *she*, a beautiful, beautiful, slim blonde. And we were all playing poker together."

"Very funny," said his mother. "Very funny indeed. But it

116

doesn't dispose of the letter. And you'd better explain it to me."

"Now listen," said his father, his voice rising in anger now. "That letter—it's—it's criminal libel, that's what it is. Whoever wrote it ought to be ashamed of themselves. Rubbish belongs in the garbage can, not in the living-room. You ought to know that."

"What letter are you talking about?" asked the boy. "Who wrote it?"

His mother suddenly thrust out the hand that clutched the yellow piece of paper, and said, "Here. Look at it and see for yourself."

"No," his father cried. "No. He's too young to see that kind of rubbish."

"He's old enough," said his mother. "Let him know about it."

The veins in his father's temples stood out more prominently than before, and he pulled his lower lip between his teeth. He looked piercingly at his son. The light from a lamp was reflected in his glasses and made his pupils look like two thin yellow points.

The boy looked down at the piece of paper his mother had handed him and began to smooth it out. On it there was a brief, clumsily-written, unsigned note. "Dear Mrs. Wright," the boy read. "You will be interested to know that your husband is carrying on with another woman. They go out together and they come back to her apartment together. You will be interested to know this."

The boy read the letter twice. His eyes widened as he read it, and he felt a strange tingling all down his back, as if tiny mice were running up and down his spine. He handed the letter back to his mother and then stared down at the floor. His body began to shiver slightly, though he wasn't cold. Words seemed to form in his throat, but his throat seemed suddenly dry and he could make no sound. Neither his father nor his mother said anything and an oppressive silence settled down over the room like a cloud.

At last his father spoke. "So now you've done it," he said. "You've let him read that piece of dirt. And now what?"

"Nothing," said his mother defiantly. "Just let him know about it, so he can make up his own mind." Her voice trailed away, as if she were unsure of herself, as if she now regretted having let the boy see the letter.

"Make up his own mind!" his father taunted her. "About what? About an anonymous letter! About a piece of malicious . . . Listen!" He turned to the boy and said almost savagely, "Somebody hasn't even the guts to sign their letter and your mother thinks it's the gospel truth."

"It isn't true, then?" the boy said, uncertain whether to believe what he had read or not. He distrusted tale-bearers. Whoever had written that letter was a rat, he thought, even if it was true.

"It's a lie," his father said. "It's a rotten lie. Let's hear no more about it. I'm sick of it all." He flung his left arm out violently, as if he were hurling something from him in disgust, and then he stalked out of the room abruptly. In the doorway he turned again and said mockingly, "Ask your mother why she doesn't have me followed if she's so sure."

His mother seemed to freeze where she stood. "Why," she said, "I—I wouldn't lower myself. . . ."

But he was already walking down the hall, into the bedroom, ignoring her.

The boy sat there, staring down at the floor, thinking, and when he glanced up he saw his mother's face looking drawn and desperate. She looked old suddenly, her hair now everywhere streaked with grey, and he felt a great pity for her.

"I'm sorry I showed you the letter, David," she said very softly. "I shouldn't have. You're too young to know about these things. But I just had to, so you'd know what I go through."

She walked over to the chesterfield and sat down beside him.

118

"You don't have to believe it," he said. "It's not true, anyway. It's a lie."

"I wish I could believe that," she said. Her voice was flat and resigned. All the anger had gone out of it. "But it's true. I know it's true."

"How do you know?" he asked.

"I just know," she said. Silently, tears came and ran down her cheeks.

"But it's only a letter," he said. "And it's not even signed."

"Go to bed now," she said, stroking his hair. "You have to go to school tomorrow."

He wished she wouldn't remind him of school, for he felt very grown up suddenly. He saw the tears streaming down her face and he almost had to cry himself. But he didn't want to cry, and he jumped up impulsively and without saying any more ran back into his room, leaving her sitting there on the chesterfield, desolate and alone.

Sleep wouldn't come. As soon as he closed his eyes the room began to see-saw violently, and he opened his eyes again and sat up in bed because he felt he would be sick otherwise. So he sat brooding on the edge of his bed, his feet dangling down to the floor, and put his hands up to his head. There was a dull pain just behind his eyeballs, and when he pressed down on his eyes with his fingers, it got worse.

He had weak eyes, like his father. Sometimes, especially toward the end of the month, his father's eyes would be red and watery, and when he came home from the office he often bathed them with boracic acid. His father was an accountant and the end of the month was his busiest time, and he often went back to the office after supper to do some more work, and sometimes he didn't come home for supper at all, but stayed downtown.

Could the letter be true, the boy thought, opening his eyes and staring out into the dark room. Suddenly he became conscious of his alarm clock. Its ticking, jerky somehow, feverish almost, seemed to pound directly in his head, and he jumped up and grabbed the alarm clock from the dresser and buried it under his pillow.

What was true and what was false? Should he believe his mother or his father? Whoever had written that letter knew his mother's name. But that meant nothing. Somebody might have a grudge against her or against his father. But what if it was true? Carrying on with another woman. That's what the letter says, he thought. And when they came together to this woman's apartment, what happened then? What did they do there?

He had never thought of his father as romantic. His hair was turning grey and he wore glasses and his voice was often raspy. He had sometimes tried to imagine how his father and his mother looked when they were going steady, long before he was born, but he could never do it. There was a picture of his mother and his father that showed them on their wedding day, with his mother all in white, holding a bouquet of roses, and his father, without glasses and much slimmer than he was now, wearing an old-fashioned tail-coat, standing beside her. But the picture had never seemed quite real to him. It was just a yellowing photograph, and the couple in it might be any couple photographed together long, long ago.

But if there was really another woman, the boy thought, what did she look like? Was she young and beautiful? She'd have to be younger and more beautiful than his mother, he thought, or else why would his father bother with her? But if she was young and beautiful, why would she bother with his father? His father said it was all a lie, but his mother said it was true. Then who was right?

In school the next day he paid hardly any attention, and was reprimanded several times. He felt very tired and depressed, but at the same time also keyed up and tense, his mind in turmoil. The hours seemed endless, and when the noon bell finally rang it sounded more sweetly than he had ever heard it before, promising deliverance.

Outside the school he wondered whether he should wait for his friend Tom, who was in another class. They lived on the same street and always walked home together. But before he could make up his mind, Tom joined him and they set off as usual. Tom began to talk about football, and they discussed their team's chances in next Saturday's game, but he couldn't get worked up about that today and suddenly he switched the subject.

"D'you remember the movie we saw about three weeks ago?" he asked.

"Which one?"

"I don't remember the name," he said. "But it was all about a man and his wife, and this man met another woman, and—well, they carried on together."

"Mhm," said Tom. "I remember. What about that movie?"

"Nothing. Except that—well, I dreamt about that picture last night, and—it sort of keeps bothering me."

"Why?"

"Because—well, I—I really don't know. Except. . . Say you get married and the girl you marry did that. You know. Carry —I mean go out with another man. But say you know nothing about it until somebody writes you a letter about it, but never signs his name."

"That's not how it was in the movie," his friend said.

"I know. But that's what I was thinking. Say it was like I was saying. What would you do?"

"I'd try to find out, naturally."

"But how?"

"Easy. I'd try and see her going out with that other man."

"And once you'd seen her?"

"I'd knock him cold," said Tom without hesitation and balled his left hand into a fist.

"And what would you do to her?"

The question seemed to stump Tom. He stopped walking

and thought for a moment. "That depends," he said, still pondering the problem. "I might take her back if I was really in love with her, but if I wasn't any more I might just kick her out."

He seemed satisfied with that solution, but David was no longer listening to him, for he suddenly knew what he must do.

When the long school day was finally over he rushed out of the building, and dashed across the street, where he caught a bus that took him straight downtown. In a drugstore exactly opposite the brick office building where his father worked he took up his vigil. He went over to the magazine racks and pretended to look at a magazine, but all the while his eyes never left the door of the building across the road. He persuaded himself that he was a detective following up some clues that might lead him to a world-shaking discovering of a great conspiracy, but he left the nature of the conspiracy deliberately vague. Desperately he tried to hide from himself the real reason why he was there, because he hated to think that he was snooping on his father. The school books he carried grew heavy and he kept shifting them from arm to arm. As the clock moved toward five, the flow of people from the building across the street increased, and the boy grew more excited and tense. At last his father came out, talking to another man, and they walked down the street together. The boy followed them at a distance. At the bus stop they parted. Then his father got on a number 6 bus, and the boy knew that he was going straight home.

Twice more he went downtown, driven by an impulse of which he was secretly ashamed, but twice more he merely saw his father catch a bus straight home.

The letter was not mentioned again. His mother and father seemed to have concluded a kind of truce, for while they did not talk much to each other, they did not quarrel either. Then one evening toward the end of the month his father remarked casually that the work was beginning to pile up and that he would stay at the office the next evening to try and clear things up.

As soon as school finished next day, the boy took a bus downtown, and after he had walked about for a while he went again into the large drugstore from which he could observe the building across the street. He stared straight out through the big plate-glass window, paying no attention to anything that was going on around him. There was a moment when he began to feel slightly ridiculous for having come at all. He no longer even pretended that he had come to make a great discovery. After a while his eyes strayed from the window and he noticed a big-hipped woman standing beside him, leafing through a magazine. When she turned the pages, he noticed that her long fingernails were painted bright red.

It was now nearly five o'clock and he began to look out for his father. At last he saw him coming out of the building, but he did not as usual walk toward the bus stop, but crossed the street and made directly for the drugstore. In consternation the boy moved toward the back of the store, trying to make himself as inconspicuous as possible amid the displays of lipsticks and hair-lotions. A clerk came up to him and asked him what he wanted, and he stammered something about chewing-gum, keeping his head turned toward the back of the store and hoping his father wouldn't see him, so he wouldn't have to make up a story of why he was here. He paid for his chewing-gum and then slowly, surreptitiously, he glanced around, and there was his father talking to the woman who'd stood beside him and whose red fingernails he had noticed. Now his father said something and they both laughed, and then his father walked over to one of the counters and bought some cigarettes. Then he went to the door, held it open for the woman, smiling at her, and they walked out of the store together, and together they went down the street.

By the time the boy came out of the store, his father and the woman had walked almost to the intersection at the end of the block, past the bus stop. Keeping his eyes on them, the boy followed them. The street was crowded, but to him it seemed as if nobody were walking there except this man and this woman, and he knew that he must not lose sight of them, but at the same time was forbidden to come close. It all seemed like a dream. Everything was clear, and everything was also very hazy, and though he felt very calm, he was also in a strange way very excited. Somewhere far away he could hear the sound of motors, and once he knew he had bumped into somebody, for he heard a man's voice saying, "Look where you're going," but he paid no attention. So he walked blindly on, never losing sight of his father and that woman, threading his way automatically through the crowd that flowed up and down the street, until at last, after what seemed an eterniy of walking, his father and the woman turned and went into a restaurant.

The boy stopped walking and began to think about what he should do. Slowly, stealthily almost, as if he were treading on forbidden ground, he walked up to the restaurant and stood on the pavement, silently pondering. From where he stood he could see the cashier's desk, and in the large window that gave upon the street there was a tank in which goldfish swam. Beyond it there moved the shadowy figures of men and women.

Was that the woman, he thought. But she was not beautiful. He could not really say what her face was like, but her figure was not very beautiful. She had large hips, and her legs were thick. He had observed them, though only from a distance. And she also had very long fingernails, and he did not like women who had very long fingernails. They reminded him of claws. But if someone had told him, when this woman came into the drugstore, that she was the woman of the anonymous letter, he would not have believed it. He did not believe it yet. Not really deep down.

But if it was true, he thought, then his father had lied to him. This realization, he knew, ought to shock him, but it didn't. It was some time now since he had ceased to believe in the all-wisdom, the all-honesty, and the all-powerfulness of parents. He had sometimes lied himself, reluctantly, unwillingly, and a sense of guilt had clung to him often, but he had got over it in a few days. Almost everybody felt forced to tell lies now and then. He knew that, and he could forgive in others what he had done himself. But she was not beautiful—this woman. She was not worth lying about. To walk with her down the street was not romantic. His mother was much more beautiful. Much more. And he felt a sudden resentment, anger even, welling up within him because his father had inflicted pain on his mother for the sake of this woman who was not even beautiful. And suddenly he wanted to be his mother's defender, the fierce champion of her cause. But what could he do except gape on impotently?

All at once, without clearly knowing what he was going to do, he found himself walking, as if in his sleep, toward the door of the restaurant. He pushed the door open and stood inside. Past the arborite-topped counter and the little black swivel-stools, past two gleaming copper coffee urns, there was a half-open folding door. Beyond it was the dining-room, and he walked uncertainly toward it. A black-coated waiter was standing there with a large menu in his hand. Did he wish to have dinner in the dining-room?

"No," he answered, shaking his head. "I'm just looking for my father."

The waiter stepped aside, and the boy walked into a long, narrow dining-room, so dimly lit that it took him a moment to make out some of the objects. All the tables had deep-red tablecloths, and on each table there stood a tall, slender vase, holding a single flower. Soft music was piped into the dining-room and mingled with the discreet clatter of knives and forks. At first he didn't see his father, but then he saw him, and began to make his way to the table where they sat—his father and that woman. He walked very slowly, because he was afraid, and secretly ashamed too. He tried to think what he should say when he came face to face with his father, when suddenly he heard his father's voice crying out, "David!"

Surprise and astonishment were mingled in the voice, and it seemed to the boy as if his name were reverberating through the dining-room. Two or three people turned to look at him as he stood silently, unable to speak, and stared at his father, and then slowly let his eyes move to the woman, who was as petrified as he and stared back at him, a half-crumbled soda cracker in a hand which seemed to have been arrested in mid-air.

The hand had red fingernails. That was what he saw first. Then he became conscious of a huge red mouth that was half open, as if the jaws had locked. Only slowly did the rest of her features become distinguishable to him. Her face, heavily rouged and powdered, seemed puffy and soft-fleshed, and the boy thought that if he stretched out his hand and touched her face, it would feel like a sponge. She wore a necklace of small pearls, and the pearls glowed warm against her throat. The necklace was the only thing about the woman that he found at all attractive.

"How did you get here?" The fury in his father's voice was not disguised by his attempt to speak calmly.

"Who is he, anyway?" the woman asked. She put the soda cracker on a plate and looked at his father, clearly puzzled.

The boy meant to tell her who he was, but he couldn't say anything. He felt hopelessly inadequate, stumbling about in a dark and fearful forest.

"You must have followed us," his father said. "You must have actually followed us."

The boy winced when he heard his father say that. He didn't want to be a sneak, slinking furtively round corners.

A waiter brushed past him, saying impatiently, "Don't block the way, please."

"Don't stand in the way, son," his father said angrily.

The woman gasped and put her hand up to her mouth. "That's not your son?" she cried.

"Yes," his father said. "Yes, it is."

The boy sat down on the chair beside his father, wishing desperately that he could vanish somehow. He became aware of a heavy lavender perfume that seemed to float in the air above the table like a low cloud. He raised his eyes and saw her big, round bosom and quickly looked away again.

"I didn't know you had a son," she stammered. "That big. You never told me."

His father ignored her. "Your mother put you up to this," he said. "Snooping about like a dog. Didn't she?"

"No," the boy cried fiercely. "No. She had nothing to do with it." He contracted his eyebrows and glowered at the woman.

"I'm going," the woman cried suddenly. "I'm not going to sit here and have him stare at me like that. What does he think I am?"

"Don't," his father said hastily. "Don't."   *

But she was already on her feet, and with a violent toss of her head she turned and hurried out of the restaurant. His father rushed after her, but she disappeared and he came back to the table alone.

"You can go home now," he said acidly, "and tell your mother how you spied on me."

The boy didn't say anything. That was another matter he would have to think about. Whether to tell his mother. Everything was all tangled up and nothing could ever be simple and straightforward again. Somehow his father had managed to hit him where he felt most vulnerable. He despised himself for having spied. There was something mean about his action. But his father had no moral right to hold it against him.

He fixed his eyes upon his father. "Is that the woman you— carry on with?" he said and stopped. He could hardly get the words out. They seemed to stick in his throat. "She looks awful," he cried viciously. "Just awful."

He knew at once, by the way his father winced and turned his eyes away, that this remark had hurt him more than if someone had thrown a stone at him.

The Wedding

Dorothy Livesay

"It's okay if she comes to see us about a month after," Barbie was telling Ken as he sat over coffee, folding the letter. "It's just, I'd like to get settled in our own place first."

"Sure. Sure. Mother'll be no bother. Why now that we're getting that upstairs apartment in the old house she'll feel right at home.... It's roomy. And uncle said we could have his day-bed for the living-room... remember?"

"Uh huh."

"Barbie, it's like I said, Mum's plain and simple... as a farm woman has to be. Loves to do things for people. And she'll enjoy the bright lights in Edmonton."

Barbie had heard that phrase before: "plain and simple... like *you*... else why would I love you so?" Well, Barbie didn't think she was all that plain... she made the most of her small blue eyes, she shampooed her blond hair every few days. She doubted, also, how he could call her "simple." But it didn't really matter. Once they were married, and on their own... with her own mother thousands of miles away, they'd be happy, happy. Yet it kept nagging her—only that evening at supper, before Ken came over, she had opened the paper and gone first to Ann Landers' column. It was all about advice to the mother-in-law. Now she wanted to read it to Ken, but she thought maybe she'd better not.

"D'you think she'll mind that I do things differently?" she asked him, snuggling down beside him on the chesterfield. He got up and turned on the TV. "Like what do you do differently?"

"Why, even little things, like how you set the table or how you make a pie."

"Listen, Babs! She's grown up. Sure, she'll likely give you her recipe for lemon pie. . . because she knows how I like it. But she won't expect you to do it that way. . . . It's just that I'm the only one, you know, the only son that she's got."

"Yes. But you are the only one *I've* got!" At that, he sat down beside her again and hugged her tight, till she forgot for a while what she had really wanted to say. Later, she tried again.

"But Ken. . ."

"Yes?"

"What about me not being Adventist?"

"You mean, what does mother say about that?"

"Uh-huh."

"Why, she knows I'm not really one, any more. She knows you've had a kind of different background, back east. . . . I told you about that girl from the farm next to ours. . . that she wanted me to marry?"

"So?"

"We had it out then. I told her straight I'd marry when I was ready and I'd marry someone that suited me. . . someone likely who would want to travel around and see more of the country than just one stretch of prairie."

"Then I guess it'll be okay."

"Sure it'll be okay. It's got to be! I respect my mother and so I know you'll respect her, too. She's pretty tolerant. . . and if you're tolerant too. . . but don't just go and memorize all the dos and don'ts about how a mother-in-law should never never never do this this this! Just let her be herself! And you be yourself."

She smiled back at him, relaxing. Maybe he *had* read the Ann Landers column! And he didn't quite agree. She saw that. She'd better forget it.

The next week was full of all the last-minute things. . . a lunch party for her at the office. . . a shower at Aunt Min's. . . the dressmaker's. . . the maid-of-honour colour scheme. Pale green, she decided. Francie was making it herself, but Barbie helped. Her own wedding dress would be white of course, with high bodice, long sleeves. "You're so slim, Barbie, those sleeves will look like wings!"

"Well, sometimes Ken calls me Angel!"

Aunt Min was arranging the reception at her house, and was getting the spare bedroom ready for Barbie's cousins, since her mother couldn't make it (it was the height of the tourist season, back east). Ken's parents had no relatives to visit with in Edmonton so they'd likely have to stay at a motel when they drove up from Lethbridge. They'd arrive just in time for the wedding service at Eastway United.

"Too bad Dad couldn't get away sooner. . . but it's just the wrong time for him, combining."

"Oh well. . . since it's not till five o'clock they can make it. You said they could, Ken."

"Uh-huh. So long as it doesn't make Dad drive too fast."

"Your Dad! Drive fast? But he's so slow and steady and quiet."

"Sure—but he undergoes a personality change, as they call it, when he's behind the wheel. . . . Oh well, Mum'll keep him in check. I bet she's busy already, getting all dolled up."

Barbie thought of her own mother. . . the widow. . . the city business woman who knew good clothes when she saw them. Yet it had been a relief to get away from her last year when she came to Edmonton to take that Dental Assistant's course. It wasn't so long ago that Barbie had confided to Francie: "My mother, she kind of glitters. If you're dressed up nice and smart she fusses over you a lot. But if you let yourself go—just padding around the kitchen in a beat-up dressing-gown—boy, she'll light into you! Seems as if she doesn't really know who you are, unless you're dressed up."

Ken's mother sure was different. She would likely copy something out of Eaton's catalogue, and then try and make it herself. Of course, she was heavy. She couldn't just walk into a store and find what would fit. Thank goodness, Barbie'd never be like that. Her own mother and Aunt Min were still as slim as slim. Barbie smoothed down her hips as she got out of bed that wedding morning. Then she took off her nightie and stood before the mirror, on tiptoe as if taking off in a ballet step. How slender she was! Would Ken like it? Would Ken...

But Ken's mother! She couldn't go on calling her that. And Ken said she mustn't call her Mrs. Olsen. "They're your new Dad and Mum," he told her.

Well, "Dad." Yes, she could think of Mr. Olsen as Dad. He was lean and thin, stoop-shouldered, weather-beaten and sort of worried-looking. She'd like to make him happy. But maybe because her own dad was dead, and she'd never called her own mother "Mum," it was harder to say it to Mrs. Olsen.

Francie thought she'd come round to it. "I think Mrs. Olsen's a real nice kind of Mum," she remembered Francie saying, that day last spring when they all drove down to Lethbridge... Francie and Peter, Barbie and Ken. And they'd all had a grand pork dinner, baked country style, and were too full to do more than sit around on the porch and talk, all evening. Mrs. Olsen had put her arms around Barbie, at bedtime, when she showed her into the little side bedroom. "I'm sure Ken'll make you happy... real happy," she whispered throatily, tears almost falling from her eyes. "He's a *good* boy."

"Yes, I know," replied Barbie, turning away to the window, throwing it open and taking in great breaths of night air.

"Oh, it smells so good on the farm. It smells so good!"

"Glad you like it," Mrs. Olsen beamed. "And I hope you'll come down real often, after you're married... and bring me a little one along too, just as soon as it's right."

"Well, I don't know if we'll hurry. . ." Barbie began, then broke off. "You know, Ken has to get through NAIT before we can afford to have a family."

"Well, the Lord will take care of it. . . you'll see. When the time comes, a woman is ready."

They kissed again, awkwardly, and Mrs. Olsen padded to the door and closed it firmly, leaving her alone. . . with Ken somewhere on the other side of the house.

It was a small wedding, but proper. Ken's friends on one side of the church, her friends on the other. Uncle Albert carried her down the aisle in fine style, though her heart was beating so fast she could hardly feel the rhythm of the wedding march. She felt as if her feet would cave in under her, any moment. Then there was Ken, quiet and steady beside her, only his eyes smiling. And before she knew it, it all went as smooth as the rehearsal. . . the ring was on her finger, she was kissed. Then out in the vestry Francie and Pete were hugging them and nearly crying, but laughing too as they all signed the register. But she was still nervous, like a string pulled too tight, when they walked back in triumph down the aisle toward the door to a clamour of tongues, jokes, kisses. . . and photographers. Her lips were set in a stiff smile, her eyes were glazed. Outside on the church steps the August evening was closing in on them, the sun fell through gold leaves throwing an aura around the white bride, the dark groom.

"Just one more," begged the photographer. So she and Ken just stood there facing each other and holding hands. As they turned away, everything suddenly breaking up, Barbie felt Mrs. Olsen pressing close to Ken. Her words seemed to hiss: "And where will you be staying tonight, dear?"

"Oh, that's not for me to say, Mum. You'll have to ask the bride!" But then here was Dad saying: "We'll only be here overnight, Ken. . . we'd kind of like to see you before we head back south."

"Sure. . . sure. Maybe tomorrow morning, Dad." Then Ken seized her arm and together, under showers of confetti, they moved toward Uncle Albert's car and led off the procession to the reception.

"O Ken!"

He kissed her, harder than ever before. "You see, Barbie, it's all right. It's all right."

"But why would your mother ask where we were going? Nobody ever asks that!"

"And nobody ever tells!" He squeezed her arm. Then they were back at Aunt Min's and it was all free and easy again, with a glass of real wine down her throat, and all the laughter and Pete making a toast to the bride. She cut the cake, circled and flew around from group to group; until Aunt Min came up to her quietly, touching her arm. "It's about time now. You just slip upstairs and change. . . the taxi'll be ready to take you to the Coachhouse Arms."

Upstairs, thank heavens, everything was packed and ready. She stepped out of the long whiteness and slipped on the pale blue suit, dabbed on lipstick in a last flurry of trembling concern. Was her hair right? Did her eyes shine?

Ken met her at the bottom of the stairs. He had already put their suitcases in the taxi. Now it was just a matter of standing at the door and waving. . . "Goodbye—Goodbye." Her Aunt Min kissed her then, and Mrs. Olsen kissed Ken. Then they fled.

"Whew! Thank God that's over."

"Was it, honest, so bad?' she asked him.

"No, not really. As long as you liked it."

"Oh yes, everything went so smooth, Ken. . . it was like in a movie!" He smiled, squeezing her hand. Then they sat silent, exhausted, washed of all emotion as the cab sped along the highway to the new motel.

At the desk, Ken knew how to do everything right. The desk clerk never winked an eye and the bellboy carried their bags up as if they had always lived there, and were no concern of his.

"I'll just step in and draw the drapes," he said, switching on the light. It was a big, fancy room with gold drapes and blue trimmings. "Want the window open, sir?"

"Oh yes," said Ken. "And thank you for your trouble." The man accepted the tip without smiling. "Goodnight, sir. Just ring if you want room service."

Barbie skipped to the window. "Look, there's a lovely moon, Ken...."

"A harvest moon... our harvest." And he suddenly lifted her up and swung her around in his arms. Then gently he laid her on the bed.

"Do we have to undress right away?"

"Of course not. Let's just lie and rest a little... shall we? In the dark?"

"Yes." He turned off the bedside lamp then lay down beside her, gently. She was grateful to him... so grateful.

It seemed they had only been shyly touching one another for a few minutes, when the phone rang.

"What's that?" She sat up rigidly, startled.

"It can't be for us. . . . Oh, the stupid desk!" He let it ring four times before he answered.

"Hello!" She could hear the woman's voice on the line... but could not make out the words. She sensed Ken standing there, tense, "Oh... did you?... well, however did you find out? . . . Oh, I see... Oh, she's fine. A bit tired, I guess. Yes. We're just resting a bit, after all the excitement. . . . Oh dear, I don't know... well, I'll have to ask her. Just a minute."

He covered the receiver with his hand, bent toward her. "It's Mum and Dad... they're here! They've taken a room here."

"Oh no-no-no-o-o."

"They want to know if they can see us for a little while... because they're driving back to Lethbridge tomorrow."

"Oh not here... not here, Ken!"

"Well, supposing I say we'll just drop down to their room for a few minutes?"

She did not answer. "Eh... Barbie? *Barbie?*"

"Okay," she whispered. She got up, to go into the bathroom

135

and wash her face.

It wasn't too bad, really, Ken kept telling her as they came back up the elevator. . . .Just a friendly hello and goodnight . . . . No harm done, eh Barbie?

She nodded. She sure wasn't going to have a fight, *now*. And just being with Ken, alone at last, that was all she wanted. And Ken spent the night making it up to her, making up for everything, everything. . . . It was okay, being married. But something you couldn't talk about—not even to Francie. Toward dawn they slept the deep, deep sleep they had longed for.

"Br-r-r-r." That goddamn phone again.

She woke up enough to say, "Don't answer! Don't answer!" He let it ring, six times. Then it stopped. By then they were both wide awake. "What time is it?"

"Eight o'clock."

"Kiss me."

It was going to be a crazy, lovely morning, she thought, her body beginning to open out, rise and fall at his least touch. Then the phone rang again.

"Oh Barbie. . . I'm so sorry, so sorry kid."

He answered it. Mrs. Olsen was asking if she could talk to her new daughter.

"Here. . . you've *got* to. . . ." He handed her the cradle. And she did it, somehow. She said hello to Mum and then to Dad and when they said they were leaving soon to go back to the farm and couldn't they all go down to the café and have breakfast together, she said yes, sure, maybe in about fifteen minutes? And then she fell back into the sheets, burrowing to hide her tears.

"That's my girl. Come on, we'll get it over with. It'll be the last time we'll see them for ages. . . ."

"I sure hope so!" But she said it only under her breath. She plunged to the bathroom for a shower, and Ken joined her and they were laughing again when they went downstairs to the dining-room. Mum beamed and said Dad would do the order-ing. . . "It's all on him" and would they like hot cakes and sau-sages? So breakfast wasn't too bad, really.

Mum did all the talking, going over every inch of the wed-ding, the guests, the food. Dad, sitting beside Barbie, was kind of heavy and silent but when the coffee came and she said: "Oh, that's just what I needed!" he patted her hand and beamed at her through his thick glasses. "I just wish I was Ken," he said, "but I guess my old car wouldn't be any good on a honeymoon."

"How is the Chev running, Dad?" Ken leaned forward, serious.

"Oh not so bad, the little we use it. She'll need a check-up soon, I guess."

"You got enough help this fall?" Ken asked him.

"I kin do with it. Could do with your hands too, if you'd like to come along!" But he wasn't serious at all, he was just jok-ing. . . she could see that. She smiled back at him and was pleased to have his rough quick kiss on her cheek as they parted, in front of the Olsen's car.

"Bye-bye."

Ken took her arm firmly as they moved back to the motel.

"That was the right thing to do. Seeing them off."

"But don't tell anybody, Ken. Honest, on our honeymoon! Don't let anybody know," she begged.

"Of course I won't. *I'd* be the joke, just think of that!"

She would have forgotten it all, perhaps, the embarrass-ment, the frustration, the fury all bottled up inside her, that wedding night. Because now it was all right, now she knew her Ken. So good a man. But at five o'clock that evening when they were down in the lounge, turning in the key and pre-paring to go out to a smart place to dinner, a policeman came up to the desk and then came alongside and touched Ken on the arm.

"Are you Mr. Olsen?"

"That's right."

"May I speak to you in private?"

"In private? Why, I just got married. . . my wife. . ."

"Very sorry, sir. But I'm afraid it's bad news."

Shaking, she sat down on a stiff chair in the lobby. Ken went back in the manager's office with the RCMP officer. It seemed ages before he came out, terribly white. . . "I've got to go," he told her. . . "down to Calgary with the police."

"You'll have to tell me!"

Ken looked back at the desk, at the policeman silent beside the manager. "It's very hard to take, Barbie." He held her hand and sat down beside it, holding her hand and rubbing it, hard. "Soon after they left Red Deer Dad must have had a blackout . . . leaped the ditch and into the other lane. A truck was coming the other way. . . his car piled into it—was found practically *under it*."

She could hardly understand. . . "You mean?"

"Dad's in hospital. . . but he rolled over on top of Mum, and the door flew open and she was thrown to the other side of the road, and down in the ditch."

"I can't believe it."

"She died right away."

"O Ken!"

She stood up and he seized her hard, pulling her close as if he was welding her to his body.

"I'm coming with you," she said. But all she could think of was that she was so small and thin, so barely able to support his weight. "If only I could put on some pounds," she thought. "Then maybe, maybe, he could rest on me."

Arm in arm they stumbled out toward the highway.

The Elevator

George Bowering

Last night I was thinking: here I sit alone in the dark room with a little portable television—we face each other with the lights of our opposite eyes, lenses bending toward each other, and in the dark I suddenly know what it is coming in rays to my eyes, thru them to my front brain—the blue light of the television, the open end of the set, it is actually a hole out of this darkness, thru all walls, into the open world. It is an extension of my eyes, the television set and the invisible camera somewhere at the other end of the wires. I can sit in my darkened room and see into the world, whichever direction I'm looking at the time. Dip—look into bedroom, young wife in silk to her knees, husband with tie hanging loose in front of him like an Anglican minister thing, talking to each other, and my ear is there too in their room, they are shouting at each other, and I see—my eye looks down at them from the ceiling and the walls have ears.

Till I thought: how still I am sitting. Sure, so I can look into the New York bedroom, zoom from airplane over the Riviera to look at bathing suits. No, because I'm unnecessary there. Can I remember turning the television on? What was I thinking at the time? Did I do it on purpose? I hesitate to think it. Am I annexed by the camera? Part of its action. The brain for its eye. Or worse. It came into the room to look across at me, then stayed there all the time while I came in and went out, it was waiting for me, always there when I came in with bottle of beer and newspaper, turning on the dial, to look at over the top of the news. Come here fingers.

"You. Television. Who needs you?"

"This is probably the salad oil you're using now."

"Salad oil. Up yours with salad oil."

The cat jumped down off the wooden table where he had been licking the dried food on yesterday's plate, and he made that throaty meow as his front feet hit the floor first, then his back ones, then gathered to spring ino a slow walk across the floor to me, tail in the air, his eyes now adding to the television, looking at me. What if television looked from a cat's eyes, in the dark? What's in that bedroom then?

The cat walked back and forth in front of me, rubbing his sides against my legs, stepping heavily with one cat foot on my toe. He was hungry. Welcome aboard. Neither of us had eaten since the day before. But for the cat it was sad. I hadn't let him out, and he'd shit in the empty bathtub again, and that was the last food he'd eaten, already hard and black in the white tub. Down the drain with you all—cat, shit, television. I got up and went out. The cat scooted out with me. As he disappeared around the corner of the house his tail went down, crouch already in the back.

"Good hunting, Janet."

Moreover thou hast taken thy sons and thy daughters whom thou hast borne unto me, and these hast thou sacrificed unto them to be devoured. Is this of thy whoredoms a small matter, that thou hast slain my children, and delivered them to cause them to pass thru the fire for them?

Ezekiel claimed that God said that to Jerusalem, but Zeke had been reading the older prophets, including several false ones, and he knew that's what the folks wanted him to say. They're still saying it, and Jerusalem among others is still doing it. I was one of the lucky children who hadn't passed thru the fire. But I'd always taken precautions. Going down in an elevator, I always flexed my knees in case of a runaway crash. But I had lately got too involved with this too—thinking too hard about a burst blood vessel in the brain can cause a burst blood vessel in the brain. Then where are you?

Outside the house, looking at the snow.

Maybe a couple quarts of fuel in the gas tank, so I started it up in the dark and drove lights out thru the streets, lighted by blue gaslights of Alberta natural gas, shining off the black steel of the car stretched out after the windshield in front of me, till I got downtown in the east end of Eighth Avenue, Sunday night, no stores open, wind in the dark flipping Saturday's paper end over end along the sidewalk till it came flat against dark-red 1910 bricks. Cornices two storeys higher jutted into the wind like leading edges of aircraft. I stopped the car and got out, thinking I was a professor, professional before I came to Calgary, so I have never walked alone in the east end winery part of town here as I had in Vancouver. And here there were no pigeons on the sidewalk.

The wind was cold, and at select corners it blew up peacock tails of snow, into the face turned the wrong way. I was the only one on the street. It was early March, no end to winter. In Vancouver the crocuses were popping up in people's lawns. I met an old man in a dark coat that came to his heels.

"Cold night," I said.

"You're right there," he said.

Without calling me sonny or young fellow. Here there is not much trouble about differing ages. The old men wear shoes with cracks down the back. The young wear boots that will eventually wear out. In the windows of the second-hand stores there are boots for $11, bright yellow next to bright yellow guitars and shiny flipdown toasters, and the big jackknife with twenty blades in various degrees of open.

I watched the man walk farther along the sidewalk, his hand up on his bald head, walking so the broken shoes wouldn't fall off his feet, and I noticed he was Chinese, the darkness rushing in to fill the place between us.

141

What is your name what is your name? Long coat frosted by the wind, moving into the loom of dark east Eighth Avenue, snow blowing into long skidded footprints, collar blown against my chin, something glanced off the side of my head and struck hard downward on my shoulder. I turned and crouched and it was dark there in front of me. I hit out and grabbed at movement, hands sliding in wet darkness as he moved away and came back. It was in his hand at the side, the thing he hit me with. My one arm was numb, hanging useless, but I stepped that way and hit him low in the middle and he spun slightly to my side and I kicked out and missed. The street was gone, the town was gone, the old Chinese man. The thing came at me again, past my face, and I knew my only way was to rush, and I swept him, so he must have been small, against the brick wall, and hit as hard as I could with my body. Then I got my arm loose and hit him as fast as I could here out of the wind. I hit and held him against the wall with my body, knee coming up against my thigh, looking for my soft groin. I saw the head for a second and smashed with my fist and back with the back of my hand, and it was hard, bones of my knuckles coming thru skin, I felt his head give way, and it hit the side of the building. He fell into the pile of snow at the base of the wall and I kicked him, but he didn't move. The thing was still in his hand. I walked away, hurting, close to the wall and toward the car. I hadn't seen his face. Old or young, I hadn't seen him. I bounced off the wall as I walked away.

In the car I sat with the engine running and fumbled with cigarettes till I got one in my mouth, the cigarette very little in my thick lips, the cold and the pain taking away all taste. I started the car and drove north, into the wind and snow.

"The temperature in Calgary a chilly three degrees," said the radio.

Chaucer. I've done Chaucer, Shakespeare, Donne, Milton, Blake. Now Pope, Wordsworth, Shelley, Browning. Professor. People outside the university called me Professor. In a town like Calgary—city they liked to call it, but the railroad tracks still cut it in half, demonstrably, like the small towns that clamp around the tracks east to west on the prairie. In the cold winter this year of February dead antelope lay frozen along a hundred miles of Alberta tracks, stiff legs pointing up at CPR passengers rolling by, eating turkey sandwiches with gravy in the dining cars. Calgary is 80 miles from the mountains and hundreds of miles from the nearest city, fed by television towers and the boxcars that carry newsprint. This university now four years old, where teachers from Germany and Chicago and Vancouver speak to inmates of Calgary about far foreign things.

That's where I was going. I had left the apartment where there was no food, and the cafés downtown were closed. Couldn't stay there now, a body lying against the wall, dead or alive probably alive, and young or old. Small, with something in his hand. The car drove me, out to the old Banff highway, turn left at the university road, around to the bus stop.

Outside the wind was stronger here on the edge of the prairie, blowing in from the Rocky Mountain Trench snow, piled for days waiting for a wind. I kept my collar up and bent over, walking to the library. My office on the fourth floor. All the lights were on; a few students would be there on the coldest night.

"Sir, I've been doing some reading."

"Good."

"I've heard that Blake was crazy. How are we supposed to read his poetry? I mean—"

"As if he was crazy. Do you think Jesus was sane? Don't underestimate Jesus, either."

Jesus tipped against his own dark satanic windmills. The glass front of the library building loomed yellow in the dark wind, snow cutting around the straight corners, glass holding it off from the books. The hole in my right shoe allowed wetness that would dye the bottom of my foot the colour of whatever sock I was wearing. In the library no-one needs shoes. Eyes.

The heavy glass door gave way to the wind half open, and I stepped into sudden heat and stillness and the drifted snow started to melt at my throat. What time is it? Ten o'clock right on. Students—young girls with ski slacks and boys in red poplin jackets—were being rushed out of the building by skinny library women anxious to be home in time for the late show. I rode the elevator upstairs to the fourth floor, my office.

The lights were bright oblongs in the ceiling, this place meant for stacks of books, but now temporarily they said full of cubicles, offices, each with bookshelves, desk, chair on wheels, blackboard, pin-board, piles of papers, ashtrays and curious oblong wastepaper buckets emptied every night by unseen janitors large windows in a room full of easy chairs, lounge, with west windows, black now, mountains in the distance, snow hissing on the glass.

I was there to do something meaningful. I sat down and unfolded a lined paper and made marks on it with a red ballpoint pen.

I opened a book and started to read a long poem by Robert Browning, but I stopped after a dozen lines—somebody in Renaissance Italy talking in long lines.

There were no footsteps in the hall. All the other offices were empty. Nobody getting ahead but me.

I smoked a cigarette and carelessly threw the burning end on the floor.

I continued marking papers in the silence that is the same anywhere there is an empty school—numbers nailed to the doors now with no meaning, blackboards within closed rooms, administrating to rows of empty seats. Chalkdust could fill the air without liming any pink lungs, like the silence, in those rooms and halls so used to the fullness of talk. I make my living by being able to talk, me so shy I could not raise my questioning hand in a classroom full of my peers, most of them stupid, afraid of getting a job. I was afraid of getting out of the wide halls and desk-filled rooms. The papers in front of my eyes on the grey-topped desk were not familiar, I had never written anything like that when I was a freshman—hesitant, awkwardly trying to fit long nouns from lecture notes into English sentences, with verbs, so shaky, so unsure. It made my heart soft as it always did. I wanted to sit close to each one, boy or girl, shadowy Walt Whitman teacher, and tell them not to try to make sense of the coincidence of bafflement in the schoolbooks of stone university, and the warm fluid that welled threateningly and buried between their soft bellies and seldom-touched thighs.

They could so obviously offer a kind of comfort to me, none of them terrified or bewildered by television; they could sit in partial observance and scrutinize the weekly trials of a blood-hand doctor, and sympathize with his patience for the sudden appearance of bottled salad oil. I was certainly gifted with speech—I could hold them, 30 at a time, and speak slowly as I wanted, authority coming from the verses in my own 170 pounds. But there were a hundred thousand television screens in Calgary, burning chill blue in dark March nights behind heavy window drapes. Could I hold up my end in a face-to-face encounter? I dropped my red pen on the paper and wheeled my chair back to the shelves of books.

There was dried blood on the knuckles of my right hand. Time to get up like the clean-conscious American on the screen, go out and like they say bathe the hand in warm water, then cold water, it closes the bloody pores. It feeds the bloody cat. I got up to leave, grabbing coat from rack and carefully fingering the thing on the edge of the door, locker of offices, opener of minds, fair friends never met.

BERGEN, NORWAY (AP)—Norwegian pigs are becoming so idle they are biting each other's tails too much and causing a rise in infectious diseases, a slaughterhouse veterinary surgeon has reported.

FALSE TEETH—Chewing Efficiency increased up to 35%. New, new.

I walked then, head down, to the elevator, flexing my knees experimentally, slightly, while walking, my worn suede shoes phantom in the empty hall. Push button. Red arrow light. Distant down sounds of lurching machinery. When it came I walked in, looking at the shape of my toes through the suede. The door whispered shut behind me. Then the lights went out, and the elevator stopped going down. My knees flexed without my thinking of it. The liquid in the top of my head dropped abruptly to earlobe level. I composed myself, and knew there was a power failure, ready to wait. I had seen it happen before; all the bright yellow lights would be gone from the windows, and the eerie spotlights with power batteries would be shining down from the high walls, a selective light in the gloom of stone corridors. My fingers had curled into a fist, slightly opening the cuts again, dab of fresh blood. It was absolutely black in the elevator.

And breathing. A scent, perfume. She was in the black too, I hadn't known there was anyone else in the elevator, someone left after the doors were locked. That had happened before, too.

The breathing was right beside me, a hand touched my chin, end of fingers, she was walking slowly in the dark, hand out in front of her, it touched me for just a second, then was snatched away. I stood still. Her breathing was not back where it started from. I was breathing too, and maybe that would make her feel all right. Because I had no idea what she looked like, how old, how big, I had my head down coming into the elevator.

"What happened?" she whispered. Her voice was very close. I wondered why.

"Power went off," I whispered back, across close darkness. "It's okay. We just have to wait."

"Couldn't we yell, or something?"

146

"Too late at night, nobody would hear us."

There was probably a janitor or a late-working librarian. Well, no sense complicating things. What good would yelling do? No amount of yelling turns on the lights. That had happened before, too. She must have moved quietly because I could feel her arm brush mine. It went away, and came back. I was comfort in the dark, I suppose, the professor. Meek and mild George Delsing puts on his magic necktie, mutters the ancient words of the scroll, and becomes: Professor-Man!

The dark man in the elevator put his arm out slowly, slowly, plunged up to the shoulder in the darkness, around probably behind her, and he drew it toward him till it touched. Her. She was wearing a coat for the cold, here unnecessary for the dark, a man could be wearing nothing; teaching in a school for blind girls, walking naked around the room, in and out among the blind alleys, in that dark, of the elevator. The girl, the woman, didn't move. Till I felt her hand on my wrist where I was holding her. I placed my other hand on her, and she came up to my neck, her hair scented under my chin. Then I felt her hands on me, here in the university, all over my body, timidly on the front of my pants, hesitating a moment on the broken skin of the knuckles.

Dew melon dew melon lying half hidden under the broad green leaves. The earth is rich.

I began taking her clothes from her, beginning with her long coat, and it was easy there in the dark, no sight of awkward lifted elbows, it was as easy as taking the linen drape from a nude sculpture. Her blouse came undone and over her shoulders, and her hands were at her skirt so that it too came off, down, easily, fell to some dark corner of the elevator. A few clasps, a few caresses of my hand on her back, her leg. My fingers went inside her panties and gently pulled them down over the round buttocks. My clothes came off easily, her hair on my naked shoulders, and we eased each other down on the pile of clothes, breath in our faces, moisture in the vales of

147

God's morning, and we fell to the deepest darkness, flowers cascading over the head of the young hero.

When my blood was moving fastest, the knuckles on my hand were hurting. Broken flesh had met broken flesh in the dark.

She whispered: "When the lights come on I will have my back to you, and you must not look at me."

"But who are you?" I asked. "I want to see you again—"

But I did as she bid. As the doors opened on the main floor, she spoke again.

"For all you will know, I might be one of the people in your class."

I waited as she asked, ten minutes, till she would be completely away from the university. My body was warm, and this would last for a few minutes in the cold night outside. In two days I would meet my class again, and the eyes of all the girls in the class would be looking at me, and they would all be listening to my voice. Wordsworth.

When I got home I had a bag full of groceries, on credit, and among them was a can of cat food. If I had a dog instead, maybe it could have licked my aching knuckles.

Polarities

Margaret Atwood

Gentle and just pleasure
It is, being human, to have won from space
This unchill, habitable interior. . . .
—Margaret Avison, "New Year's Poem"

He hadn't seen her around for a week, which was unusual: he asked her if she'd been sick.

"No," she said, "working." She always spoke of what she had been doing with organizational, almost military briskness. She had a little packsack in which she carried around her books and notebooks. To Morrison, whose mind shambled from one thing to another, picking up, fingering, setting down, she was a small model of the kind of efficiency he ought to be displaying more of. Perhaps that was why he had never wanted to touch her: he liked women who were not necessarily more stupid but lazier than himself. Sloth aroused him: a girl's unwashed dishes were an invitation to laxity and indulgence.

She marched beside him along the corridor and down the stairs, her short clipped steps syncopating with his own lanky strides. As they descended, the smell of straw, droppings and formaldehyde grew stronger: a colony of overflow experimental mice from the science building lived in the cellar. When he saw that she was leaving the building too and probably going home he offered her a lift.

"Only if you're heading that way anyway." Louise didn't accept favours, she had made that clear from the start. When he'd asked her if she wanted to take in a film with him she said, "Only if you let me pay for my own ticket." If she had been taller he might have found this threatening.

It was colder, the weak red sun almost down, the snow purpling and creaky. She jumped up and down beside his car till he got the plug-in engine heater untangled and the door opened, her head coming out of the enormous second-hand fur coat she wore, like a gopher's out of its burrow. He had seen a lot of gophers on the drive across, many of them dead; one he had killed himself, an accident, it had dived practically under the car wheels. The car itself hadn't held up either: by the time he made it to the outskirts—though later he realized that this was in fact the city—a fender had come off and the ignition was failing. He'd had to junk it, and decided stoically to do without a car until he found he couldn't.

He swung the car onto the driveway that led from the university. It bumped as though crossing a metal-plated bridge: the tires were angular from the cold, the motor sluggish. He should take the car for long drives more often, it was getting stale. Louise was talking more than she normally did, she was excited about something. Two of her students had been giving her a hassle, but she told them they didn't have to come to class. "It's your heads, not mine." She knew she had won, they would shape up, they would contribute. Morrison was not up on the theories of group dynamics, he liked the old way: you taught the subject and forgot about them as people. It disconcerted him when they slouched into his office and mumbled at him, fidgeting and self-conscious, about their fathers or their love lives. He didn't tell them about his father or his love life and he wished they would observe the same reticence, though they seemed to think they had to do it in order to get extensions on their term papers. At the beginning of the year one of his sudents had wanted the class to sit in a circle but luckily the rest of them had preferred straight lines.

"It's right here," she said; he had been driving past it. He crunched the car to a halt, fender against the rock bank, snowbank. Here they did not take the snow away; they spread sand on it, layer by layer as it fell, confident there would be no thaw.

"It's finished; you can come in and see it," she said, suggesting but really demanding.

"What's finished?" he asked. He hadn't been paying attention.

"I told you. My place, my apartment, that's what I've been working on."

The house was one of the featureless two-storey boxes thrown up by the streetful in the years after the war when there was a housing boom and materials were scarce. It was stuccoed with a greyish gravel Morrison found spiritually depleting. There were a few older houses, but they were quickly being torn down by developers; soon the city would have no visible past at all. Everything else was high-rises, or worse, low barrack-shaped multiple housing units, cheaply tacked together. Sometimes the rows of flimsy buildings—snow on their roofs, rootless white faces peering suspiciously out through their windows, kids' toys scattered like trash on the walks—reminded him of old photographs he had seen of mining camps. They were the houses of people who did not expect to be living in them for long.

Her apartment was in the basement. As they went around to the back and down the stairs, avoiding on the landing a newspaper spread with the overshoes and boots of the family living upstairs, Morrison remembered vividly and with a recurrence of panic, his own search for a place, a roof, a container, his trudges from address to address, his tours of clammy, bin-like cellars hastily done up by the owners in a vinyl tile and sheets of cheap panelling to take advantage of the student inflow and the housing squeeze. He'd known he would never survive a winter buried like that or closed in one of the glass-sided cardboard-carton apartment buildings. Were there no real ones, mellowed, interesting, possible? Finally he had come upon an available second storey; the house was pink gravel instead of grey, the filth was daunting and the landlady querulous, but he had taken it immediately just to be able to open a window and look out.

He had not known what to expect of Louise's room. He had never visualized her as living anywhere, even though he had collected her and dropped her off outside the house a number of times.

"I finished the bookshelves yesterday," she said, waving at a wall-length structure of varnished boards and cement blocks. "Sit down, I'll make you some cocoa." She went into the kitchen, still with her fur coat on, and Morrison sat down in the leatherette swivel armchair. He swivelled, surveying, comparing it with the kind of interior he thought of himself as inhabiting but never got around to assembling.

She had obviously put a lot of energy into it, but the result was less like a room than like several rooms, pieces of which had been cut out and pasted onto one another. He could not decide what created this effect: it was the same unity in diversity he had found in the motels on the way across, the modernish furniture, the conventional framed northern landscapes on the walls. But her table was ersatz Victorian and the prints Picasso. The bed was concealed behind a partly-drawn dyed burlap curtain at the end of the room, but visible on the bedside rug were two light-blue fuzzy slippers that startled, almost shocked him: they were so unlike her.

Louise brought the cocoa and sat down opposite him on the floor. They talked as usual about the city: they were both still looking for things to do, a quest based on their shared eastern assumption that cities ought to be entertaining. It was this rather than mutual attraction which led them to spend as much time together as they had; most of the others were married or had been here too long and had given up.

The films changed slowly; the one theatre, with its outdated popular comedies, they had sneered at. They had gone to the opera together when it had come, though: local chorus and imported stars— *Lucia*, it had been, and really quite well done considering. At intermission Morrison had glanced around at the silent, chunky audience in the lobby, some of the women still in early sixties pointed-toe spike heels, and murmured to Louise that it was like tourist brochures from Russia.

One Sunday before the snow came they had gone for an impromptu drive; at her suggestion they had aimed for the zoo twenty miles from the city. After they made it through the oil derricks there had been trees; not the right kind of trees—he had felt as he had on the way across that the land was keeping itself apart from him, not letting him in; there had to be more to it than this repetitive, noncommittal drabness—but still trees; and the zoo once they reached it was spacious, the animals kept in enclosures large enough for them to run in and even hide if they wanted to.

Louise had been there before—how, since she had no car, he didn't ask—and showed him around. "They choose animals that can survive the winter," she said. "It's open all year. They don't even know they're in a zoo." She pointed out the artificial mountain made of cement blocks for the mountain goats to climb on. Morrison didn't as a rule like any animal bigger and wilder than a cat, but these kept far enough away to be tolerable.

That day she had told him a little about herself, a departure: mostly she talked about her work. She had travelled in Europe, she told him, and had spent a year studying in England.

"What are you doing here?" he had asked.

She shrugged. "They gave me money; nobody else would."

Essentially it was his reason too. It wasn't the draft; he was really over-age, though here they kept wanting to think he was a dodger, it made his presence more acceptable to them. The job market had been tight back in the States and also, when he tried later, in what they called here the East. But in fairness it hadn't been only the money or the dismalness of the situation back home. He had wanted something else, some adventure; he felt he might learn something new. He had thought the city would be near the mountains. But except for the raw gulley through which the brownish river curved it was flat.

"I don't want you to think of it as typical," Louise was saying. "You ought to see Montreal."

"Are *you* typical?" he asked.

She laughed. "None of us are typical, or do we all look alike to you? I'm not typical, I'm all-inclusive."

She let her fur coat fall down from around her shoulders as she said this, and he wondered again whether he was expected to make a move, to approach her. He ought to approach someone or something, he was beginning to feel isolated inside his clothes and skin. His students were out of the question; besides, they were so thick, so impermeable; the girls, even the more slender ones, made him think of slabs of substance white and congealed, like lard; and the other single women on staff were much older than he was; in them Louise's briskness had degenerated into a pinpointing, impaling quality.

There must be a place where he could meet someone, some nice loosely-structured girl with ungroomed, seedy breasts, more thing than idea, slovenly and gratuitous. They existed, he was familiar with them from what he had begun to think of as his previous life, but he had not kept in touch with any of them. They had all been good at first but even the sloppiest had in time come to require something from him he thought he was not yet ready to give: they wanted him to be in love with them, an exertion of the mind too strenuous for him to undertake. His mind, he felt, was needed for other things, though he wasn't quite sure what they were. He was tasting, exploring: goals would come later.

Louise wasn't at all like them; she would never lend him her body for nothing, even temporarily, though she had the fur spread out around her now like a rug and had raised one corduroy-trousered knee, letting him see in profile the taut bulge of her somewhat muscular thigh. She probably went skiing and ice skating. He imagined his long body locked in that athletic, chilly grip, his eyes darkened by fur. Not yet, he thought, raising his half-full cocoa cup between them. I can do without, I don't need it yet.

It was the weekend and Morrison was painting his apartment as he habitually did on weekends; he had been at it off and on since he moved in.

"You'll have to have it painted, of course," he'd said smoothly to the landlady when inspecting it, but he had already shown himself too eager and she'd outfoxed him. "Well, I don't know, there's another boy wants it says he'll paint it himself. . ." So of course Morrison had to say he would too. This was the third coat.

Morrison's vision of wall-painting had been drawn from the paint ads—spot-free housewives gliding it on, one-handed and smiling—but it was not so easy. The paint got on the floor, on the furniture, in his hair. Before he could even begin he had to cart out the accumulated discards of several generations of previous tenants: baby clothes, old snapshots, an inner tube, heaps of empty liquor bottles, and (intriguingly) a silk parachute. Messiness interested him only in women, he could not live surrounded by it himself.

One wall of the living-room had been pink, one green, one orange and one black. He was painting them white. The last tenants, a group of Nigerian students, had left weird magic-looking murals on the walls: a sort of swamp, in black on the orange wall, and an upright shape, in pink on the green wall, was either a very poorly-done Christ Child or—could it be?—an erect penis with a halo around it. Morrison painted these two walls first, but it made him uneasy to know the pictures were still underneath the paint. Sometimes as he rollered his way around the room he wondered what the Nigerians had thought the first time it hit 40 below.

The landlady seemed to prefer foreign students, probably because they were afraid to complain: she had been aggrieved when Morrison had demanded a real lock for his door. The cellar was a warren of cubbyholes; he was not sure yet exactly who lived in them. Soon after he had moved in a Korean had appeared at his door, hopefully smiling.

"My name Robert. I have no friend."

"I'm sorry," Morrison had said, "some other time, okay? I have a lot of work to do." He was nice enough no doubt but Morrison didn't want to get involved with someone he didn't know; and he did have work to do. He felt picayune about it later when he discovered the Korean had a wife and child down in his cubbyhole with him; often in the fall they had put fish out to dry, stringing them on the clotheslines where they twirled in the wind like plastic gas-station decorations.

He was doing the ceiling, craning his neck, with the latex oozing down the handle of the roller onto his arm, when the buzzer went. He almost hoped it was the Korean, he seldom saw anyone on the weekends. But it was Louise.

"Hi," he said, surprised.

"I just thought I'd drop in," she said. "I don't use the phone any more."

"I'm painting," he said, partly as an excuse: he wasn't sure he wanted her in the house. What would she demand from him?

"Can I help?" she asked, as though it was a big treat.

"Actually I was about to stop for the day," he lied. He knew she would be better at it than he was.

He made tea in the kitchen and she sat at the table and watched him.

"I came to talk about Blake," she said. "I have to do a paper." Unlike him she was only a Graduate Assistant, she was taking a course.

"What aspect?" Morrison asked, not interested. Blake wasn't his field. He didn't mind the earlier lyrics but the prophecies bored him and the extravagant letters in which Blake called his friends angels of light and vilified his enemies he found in bad taste.

"We each have to analyse one poem in *Songs of Experience*. I'm supposed to do the 'Nurse's Song.' But they don't know what's going on in that course, he doesn't know what's going on. I've been trying to get through to them but they're all doing the one-up thing, they don't know what's happening. They sit there and pull each other's papers apart, I mean, they don't know what poetry's supposed to be *for*." She wasn't drinking her tea.

"When's it due?" he asked, keeping on neutral ground.

"Next week. But I'm not going to do it, not the way *they* want. I'm giving them one of my own poems. That says it all. I mean, if they have to read one right there in the class they'll get what Blake was trying to do with *cadences*. I'm getting it xeroxed." She hesitated, less sure of herself. "Do you think that'll be all right?"

Morrison wondered what he would do if one of his own students tried such a ploy. He hadn't thought of Louise as the poetry-writing type. "Have you checked with the professor about it?"

"I try to talk to him," she said, "I try to *help* him but I can't get *through* to him. If they don't get what I mean though I'll know they're all phonies and I can just walk out." She was twisting her cup on the table top, her lips were trembling.

Morrison felt his loyalties were being divided; also he didn't want her to cry, that would involve dangerous comforting pats, even an arm around her shoulder. He tried to shut out an involuntary quick image of himself on top of her in the middle of the kitchen floor, getting white latex all over her fur. *Not today*, his mind commanded, pleaded.

As if in answer the reverberations of an organ boomed from beneath their feet, accompanied by a high quavering voice: *Rock of a-ges, cleft for me... Let me HIIIDE myself...* Louise took it as a signal. "I have to go," she said. She got up and went out as abruptly as she had come, thanking him perfunctorily for the tea she hadn't drunk.

The organ was a Hammond, owned by the woman down-stairs, a native. When her husband and nubile child were home she shouted at them. The rest of the time she ran the vacuum cleaner or picked out hymn tunes and old favourites on the organ with two fingers, singing to herself. The organ was to Morrison the most annoying. At first he tried to ignore it; then he put on opera records, attempting to drown it out. Finally he recorded it with his tape recorder. When the noise got too aggravating he would aim the speakers down the hot air regis-ter and run the tape through as loudly as possible. It gave him a sense of participation, of control.

He did this now, admiring the way the tape clashed with what she was currently playing: *Whispering Hope* with an overlay of *Annie Laurie, The Last Rose of Summer* counter-pointing *Come to the Church in the Wildwood.* He was sur-prised at how much he was able to hate her: he had only seen her once, looking balefully out at him from between her hide-ous flowered drapes as he wallowed through the snow on his way to the garage. Her husband was supposed to keep the walk shovelled but didn't.

Louise came back the next day before Morrison was up. He was awake but he could tell by the chill in the room—his breath was visible—and by the faint smell of oil that some-thing had gone wrong with the furnace again. It was less trouble to stay in bed, at least till the sun was well risen, than to get up and try the various ways of keeping warm.

When the buzzer went he dragged a blanket around himself and stumbled to the door.

"I thought of something," Louise said tragically. She was in the door before he could fend her off.

"I'm afraid it's cold in here," he said.

"I had to come over and tell you. I don't use the phone any more. You should have yours taken out."

She stomped the snow from her boots while Morrison retreated into the living-room. There was a thick crust of frost on the insides of the windows; he lit the gas fireplace. Louise stalked impatiently around the uncarpeted floor.

"You aren't listening," she said. He looked out obediently at her from his blanket. "What I thought of is this: *The city has no right to be here.* I mean, why is it? No city should be here, this far north; it isn't even on a lake or an important river, even. Why is it here?" She clasped her hands, gazing at him as though everything depended on his answer.

Morrison, standing on one bare foot, reflected that he had often since his arrival asked himself the same question. "It started as a trading-post," he said, shivering.

"But it doesn't *look* like one. It doesn't look like anything, it doesn't *have* anything, it could be anywhere. Why is it *here?*" She implored; she even clutched a corner of his blanket.

Morrison shied away. "Look," he said, "do you mind if I get some clothes on?"

"Which room are they in?" she asked suspiciously.

"The bedroom," he said.

"That's all right. That room's all right," she said.

Contrary to his fear she made no attempt to follow him in. When he was dressed he returned to find her sitting on the floor with a piece of paper. "We have to complete the circle," she said. "We need the others."

"What others?" He decided she was overtired, she had been working too hard: she had deep red blotches around her eyes and the rest of her face was pale green.

"I'll draw you a diagram of it," she said. But instead she sat on the floor, jabbing at the paper with the pencil point. "I wanted to work out my own system," she said plaintively, "but they wouldn't let me." A tear slid down her cheek.

"Maybe you need to talk to someone," Morrison said, over-casually.

She raised her head. "But I'm talking to you. Oh," she said, reverting to her office voice, "you mean a shrink. I saw one earlier. He said I was very sane and a genius. He took a reading of my head: he said the patterns in my brain are the same as Julius Caesar's, only his were military and mine are creative." She started jabbing with the pencil again.

"I'll make you a peanut butter sandwich," Morrison said, offering the only thing he himself wanted right then. It did not occur to him until months later when he was remembering it to ask himself how anyone could have known about the patterns in Julius Caesar's brain. At the moment he was wondering whether Louise might not in fact be a genius. He felt helpless because of his own inability to respond; she would think him as obtuse as the others, whoever they were.

At first she did not want him to go into the kitchen: she knew the telephone was in there. But he promised not to use it. When he came out again with a piece of bread on which he had spread with difficulty the gelid peanut butter, she was curled inside her coat in front of the fire, sleeping. He laid the bread gently beside her as if leaving crumbs on a stump for unseen animals. Then he changed his mind, retrieved it, took it on tiptoe into the kitchen and ate it himself. He turned on the oven, opened the oven door, wrapped himself in a blanket from the bedroom and read Marvell.

She slept for nearly three hours; he didn't hear her get up. She appeared in the kitchen doorway, looking much better, though a greyish-green pallor still lingered around her mouth and eyes.

"That was just what I needed," she said in her old brisk voice. "Now I must be off; I have lots of work to do." Morrison took his feet off the stove and saw her to the door.

"Don't fall," he called after her cheerfully as she went down the steep wooden steps, her feet hidden under the rim of her coat. The steps were icy, he didn't keep them cleared properly. His landlady was afraid someone would slip on them and sue her.

At the bottom Louise turned and waved at him. The air was

thickening with ice fog, frozen water particles held in suspension; if you ran a horse in it, they'd told him, the ice pierced its lungs and it bled to death. But they hadn't told him that till after he'd trotted to the university in it one morning when the car wouldn't start and complained aloud in the coffee room about the sharp pains in his chest.

He watched her out of sight around the corner of the house. Then he went back to the living-room with a sense of recapturing lost territory. Her pencil and the paper she had used, covered with dots and slashing marks, an undeciphered code, were still by the fireplace. He started to crumple the paper up, but instead folded it carefully and put it on the mantelpiece where he kept his unanswered letters. After that he paced the apartment, conscious of his own work awaiting him but feeling as though he had nothing to do.

Half an hour later she was back again; he discovered he had been expecting her. Her face was mournful, all its lines led downward as though tiny hands were pulling at the jaw-line skin.

"Oh, you have to come out," she said, pleading. "You have to come out, there's too much fog."

"Why don't you come in?" Morrison said. That would be easier to handle. Maybe she'd been into something, if that was all it was he could wait it out. He'd been cautious himself, it was a small place and the local pusher was likely to be one of your own students; also he had no desire to reduce his mind to oatmeal mush.

"No," she said, "I can't go through this door any more. It's wrong. You have to come out." Her face became crafty, as though she was planning. "It will do you good to get out for a walk," she said reasonably.

She was right, he didn't get enough exercise. He pulled on his heavy boots and went to find his coat.

As they creaked and slid along the street Louise was pleased with herself, triumphant; she walked slightly ahead of him as if determined to keep the lead. The ice fog surrounded them, deadened their voices; it was crystallizing like a growth of spruce needles on the telephone wires and the branches of the few trees which he could not help thinking of as stunted, though to the natives, he supposed, they must represent the normal size for trees. He took care not to breathe too deeply. A flock of grosbeaks whirred and shrilled up ahead, picking the last few red berries from a mountain ash.

"I'm glad it isn't sunny," Louise said. "The sun was burning out the cells in my brain, but I feel a lot better now."

Morrison glanced at the sky. The sun was up there somewhere, marked by a pale spot in the otherwise evenly spread grey. He checked an impulse to shield his eyes and thereby protect his brain cells: he realized it was an attempt to suppress the undesired knowledge that Louise was disturbed or, out with it, she was crazy.

"Living here isn't so bad," Louise said, skipping girlishly on the hard-packed snow. "You just have to have inner resources. I'm glad I have them; I think I have more than you, Morrison, I have more than most people. That's what I said to myself when I moved here."

"Where are we going?" Morrison asked when they had accomplished several blocks. She had taken him west, along a street he was not familiar with, or was it the fog?

"To find others, of course," she said, glancing back at him contemptuously. "We have to complete the circle."

Morrison followed without protest; he was relieved there would soon be others.

She stopped in front of a medium-tall high-rise. "They're inside," she said. Morrison went toward the front door, but she tugged at his arm.

"You can't go in that door," she said, "it's facing the wrong way. It's the wrong door."

"What's the matter with it?" Morrison asked. It might be the wrong door (and the longer he looked at it, plate glass and shining evilly, the more he saw what she meant), but it was the only one.

"It faces east," she said. "Don't you know? The city is polarized north and south; the river splits it in two; the poles are the gas plant and the power plant. Haven't you ever noticed the bridge joins them together? That's how the current gets across. We have to keep the poles in our brains lined up with the poles of the city, that's what Blake's poetry is all about. You can't break the current."

"Then how do we get in?" he said. She sat down in the snow; he was afraid again she was going to cry.

"Listen," he said hastily, "I'll go in the door sideways and bring them out; that way I won't break the current. You won't have to go through the door at all. Who are they?" he asked as an afterthought.

When he recognized the name he was elated: she wasn't insane after all, the people were real, she had a purpose and a plan. This was probably just an elaborate way of arranging to see her friends.

They were the Jamiesons; Dave was one of those with whom Morrison had exchanged pleasantries in the hallways but nothing further. His wife had a recent baby. Morrison found them in their Saturday shirts and jeans; he tried to explain what he wanted, which was difficult because he wasn't sure. Finally he said he needed help. Only Dave could come, the wife had to stay behind with the baby.

"I hardly know Louise, you know," Dave volunteered in the elevator.

"Neither do I," said Morrison.

Louise was waiting behind a short fir tree on the front lawn. She came out when she saw them. "Where's the baby?" she said. "We need the baby to complete the circle. We *need* the baby. Don't you know the country will split apart without it?" She stamped her foot at them angrily.

"We can come back for it," Morrison said, which pacified

163

her. She said there were only two others they had to collect; she explained that they needed people from both sides of the river. Dave Jamieson suggested they take his car, but Louise was now off cars: they were as bad as telephones, they had no fixed directions. She wanted to walk. At last they persuaded her onto the bus, pointing out that it ran north and south. She had to make certain first that it ran over the right bridge, the one near the gas plant.

The other people Louise had named lived in an apartment overlooking the river. She seemed to have picked them not because they were special friends but because from their living-room, which she had been in once, both the gas plant and the power plant were visible. The apartment door faced south; Louise entered the building with no hesitation.

Morrison was not overjoyed with Louise's choice. This couple was foremost among the local anti-Americans: he had to endure Paul's bitter sallies almost daily in the coffee room, while Leota at staff parties had a way of running on in his presence about the wicked Americans and then turning to him and saying, mouth but not eyes gushing, "Oh, but I forgot—*you're* an American." He had found the best defence was to agree. "You Yanks are coming up and taking all our jobs," Paul would say, and Morrison would nod affably. "That's right, you shouldn't let it happen. I wonder why you hired me?" Leota would start in about how the Americans were buying up all the industry, and Morrison would say, "Yes, it's a shame. Why are you selling it to us?' He saw their point, of course, but he wasn't Procter and Gamble. What did they want him to do? What were they doing themselves, come to think of it? But Paul had once broken down after too many beers in the Faculty Club and confided that Leota had been thin when he married her but now she was fat. Morrison held the memory of that confession as a kind of hostage.

He had to admit though that on this occasion Paul was much more efficient than he himself was capable of being. Paul saw at once what it had taken Morrison hours, perhaps weeks, to see: that something was wrong with Louise. Leota decoyed her into the kitchen with a glass of milk while Paul conspired single-handedly in the living-room.

"She's crazy as a coot. We've got to get her to the loony bin. We'll pretend to go along with her, this circle business, and when we get her downstairs we'll grab her and stuff her into my car. How long has this been going on?"

Morrison didn't like the sound of the words "grab" and "stuff." "She won't go in cars," he said.

"Hell," said Paul, "I'm not walking in this bloody weather. Besides, it's miles. We'll use force if necessary." He thrust a quick beer at each of them and when he judged they ought to have finished they all went into the kitchen and Paul carefully told Louise that it was time to go.

"Where?" Louise asked. She scanned their faces; she could tell they were up to something. Morrison felt guilt seeping into his eyes and turned his head away.

"To get the baby," Paul said. "Then we can form the circle."

Louise looked at him strangely. "What baby? What circle?" she said, testing him.

"*You* know," Paul said persuasively. After a moment she put down her glass of milk, still almost full, and said she was ready.

At the car she balked. "Not in there," she said, planting her feet. "I'm not going in there." When Paul gripped her arm and said, soothingly and menacingly, "Now be a good girl," she broke away from him and ran down the street, stumbling and sliding. Morrison didn't have the heart to run after her; already he felt like a traitor. He watched stupidly while Dave and Paul chased after her, catching her at last and half-carrying her back; they held her wriggling and kicking inside her fur coat as though it was a sack. Their breath came out in white spurts.

"Open the back door, Morrison," Paul said, sergeant-like,

giving him a scornful glance as though he was good for nothing else. Morrison obeyed and Louise was thrust in, Dave holding her more or less by the scruff of the neck and Paul picking up her feet. She did not resist as much as Morrison expected. He got in on one side of her; Dave was on the other. Leota, who had waddled down belatedly, had reached the front seat; once they were in motion she turned around and made false, cheering-up noises at Louise.

"Where are they taking me?" Louise whispered to Morrison. "It's to the hospital, isn't it?" She was almost hopeful, perhaps she had been depending on them to do this. She snuggled close to Morrison, rubbing her thigh against his; he tried not to move away.

As they reached the outskirts she whispered to him again. "This is silly, Morrison. They're being silly, aren't they? When we get to the next stoplight, open the door on your side and we'll jump out and run away. We'll go to my place."

Morrison smiled wanly at her, but he was almost inclined to try it. Although he knew he couldn't do anything to help her and did not want the responsibility anyway, he also didn't want his mind burdened with whatever was going to happen to her next. He felt like someone appointed to a firing squad: it was not his choice, it was his duty, no-one could blame him.

There was less ice fog now. The day was turning greyer, bluer: they were moving east, away from the sun. The mental clinic was outside the city, reached by a curving, expressionless driveway. The buildings were the same assemblage of disparate once-recent styles as those at the university: the same jarring fragmentation of space, the same dismal failure at modishness. Government institutions, Morrison thought; they were probably done by the same architect.

Louise was calm as they went to the Reception entrance. Inside was a glass-fronted cubicle, decorated with rudimentary Christmas bells cut from red and green construction paper. Louise stood quietly, listening with an amused, tolerant smile, while Paul talked with the receptionist; but when a young intern appeared she said, "I must apologize for my friends; they've been drinking and they're trying to play a practical joke on me."

The intern frowned inquiringly. Paul blustered, relating Louise's theories of the circle and the poles. She denied everything and told the intern he should call the police; a joke was a joke but this was a misuse of public property.

Paul appealed to Morrison as her closest friend. "Well," Morrison hedged, "she *was* acting a little strange, but maybe not enough to. . ." His eyes trailed off to the imitation-modern interior, the corridors leading off into God knew where. Along one of the corridors a listless figure shuffled.

Louise was carrying it off so well, she was so cool, she had the intern almost convinced; but when she saw she was winning she lost her grip. Giving Paul a playful shove on the chest, she said, "We don't need *your* kind here. *You* won't get into the circle." She turned to the intern and said gravely, "Now I have to go. My work is very important, you know. I'm preventing the civil war."

After she had been registered, her few valuables taken from her and locked in the safe ("So they won't be stolen by the patients," the receptionist said), her house keys delivered to Morrison at her request, she disappeared down one of the corridors between two interns. She was not crying, nor did she say goodbye to any of them, though she gave Morrison a dignified, freezing nod. "I expect you to bring my notebook to me," she said with a pronounced English accent. "The black one, I need it. You'll find it on my desk. And I'll need some underwear. Leota can bring that."

Morrison, shamed and remorseful, promised he would visit.

When they got back to the city they dropped Dave Jamieson off at his place; then the three of them had pizza and cokes together. Paul and Leota were friendlier than usual: they wanted to find out more. They leaned across the table, questioning, avid, prying; they were enjoying it. This, he realized, was for them the kind of entertainment the city could best afford.

Afterward they all went to Louise's cellar to gather up for her those shreds of her life she had asked them to allow her. Leota found the underwear (surprisingly frilly, most of it purple and black) after an indecently long search through Louise's bureau drawers; he and Paul tried to decide which of the black notebooks on her desk she would want. There were eight or nine of them; Paul opened a few and read excerpts at random, though Morrison protested weakly. References to the poles and the circle dated back several months; before he had known her, Morrison thought.

In her notebooks Louise had been working out her private system, in aphorisms and short poems which were throughly sane in themselves but which taken together were not; though, Morrison reflected, the only difference is that she's taken as real what the rest of us pretend is only metaphorical. Between the aphorisms were little sketches like wiring diagrams, quotations from the English poets, and long detailed analyses of her acquaintances at the university.

"Here's you, Morrison," Paul said with a relishing chuckle. " 'Morrison is not a complete person. He needs to be completed, he refuses to admit his body is part of his mind. He can be in the circle possibly, but only if he will surrender his role as a fragment and show himself willing to merge with the greater whole.' Boy, she must've been nutty for months."

They were violating her, entering her privacy against her will. "Put that away," Morrison said, more sharply than he ordinarily dared to speak to Paul. "We'll take the half-empty notebook, that must be the one she meant."

There were a dozen or so library books scattered around the room, some overdue: geology and history for the most part, and one volume of Blake. Leota volunteered to take them back.

As he was about to slip the catch on the inside lock Morrison glanced once more around the room. He could see now where it got its air of pastiche: the bookcase was a copy of the one in Paul's living-room, the prints and the table were almost identical with those at the Jamiesons'. Other details stirred dim images of objects half-noted in the various houses, at the various but nearly identical get-acquainted parties. Poor Louise had been trying to construct herself out of the other people she had met. Only from himself had she taken nothing; thinking of his chill interior, embryonic and blighted, he realized it had nothing for her to take.

He kept his promise and went to see her. His first visit was made wtih Paul and Leota, but he sensed their resentment: they seemed to think their countrywoman should be permitted to go mad without witness or participation by any Yanks. After that he drove out by himself in his own car.

On his second visit Louise initially seemed better. They met in a cramped cubicle furnished with two chairs; Louise sat on the edge of hers, her hands folded in her lap, her face polite, withholding. Her English accent was still noticeable, though hard rs surfaced in it from time to time. She was having a good rest, she said; the food was all right and she had met some nice people but she was eager to get back to her work; she worried about who was looking after her students.

"I guess I said some pretty crazy things to you," she smiled.

"Well. . ." Morrison stalled. He was pleased by this sign of her recovery.

"I had it all wrong. I thought I could put the country together by joining the two halves of the city into a circle, using the magnetic currents." She gave a small disparaging laugh, then dropped her voice. "What I hadn't figured out though was that the currents don't flow north and south, like the bridge. They flow east and west, like the river. And I didn't *need* to form the circle out of a bunch of incomplete segments. I didn't even need the baby. I mean," she said in a serious whis-

169

per, dropping her accent completely, "I *am* the circle. I have the poles within myself. What I have to do is keep myself in one piece, it *depends* on me."

At the desk he tried to find out what was officially wrong with Louise but they would not tell him anything, it wasn't the policy.

On his next visit she spoke to him almost the whole time in what to his untrained ear sounded like perfectly fluent French. Her mother was a French Protestant, she told him, her father an English Catholic. *"Je peux vous dire tout ceci,"* she said, *"parce que vous êtes américain.* You are outside it." To Morrison this explained a lot; but the next time she claimed to be the daughter of an Italian opera singer and a Nazi general. "Though I also have some Jewish blood," she added hastily. She was tense and kept standing up and sitting down again, crossing and re-crossing her legs; she would not look at Morrison directly but addressed her staccato remarks to the centre of his chest.

After this Morrison stayed away for a couple of weeks. He did not think his visits were doing either of them any good, and he had papers to mark. He occupied himself once more with the painting of his apartment and the organ music of the woman downstairs; he shovelled his steps and put salt on them to melt the ice. His landlady, uneasy because she had still not supplied him with a lock, unexpectedly had him to tea, and the tacky plastic grotesqueries of her interior decoration fueled his reveries for a while. The one good thing in her bogus ranch-style bungalow had been an egg, blown and painted in the Ukrainian manner, but she had dismissed it as ordinary, asking him to admire instead a cake of soap stuck with artificial flowers to resemble a flowerpot; she had got the idea out of a magazine. The Korean came up one evening to ask him about life insurance.

But the thought of Louise out there in the windswept institution grounds with nothing and no-one she knew bothered him in twinges, like a mental neuralgia, goading him finally into the section of the city that passed for downtown: he would buy her a gift. He selected a small box of water-colour paints: she ought to have something to do. He was intending to mail it, but sooner than he expected he found himself again on the wide deserted entrance driveway.

They met once more in the visitors' cubicle. He was alarmed by the change in her: she had put on weight, her muscles had slackened, her breasts dropped. Instead of sitting rigidly as she had done before, she sprawled in the chair, legs apart, arms hanging; her hair was dull and practically uncombed. She was wearing a short skirt and purple stockings, in one of which there was a run. Trying not to stare at this run and at the white, loose thigh flesh it revealed, Morrison had the first unmistakeably physical stirrings of response he had ever felt toward her.

"They have me on a different drug," she said. "The other one was having the wrong effect. I was allergic to it." She mentioned that someone had stolen her hairbrush, but when he offered to bring her another one she said it didn't matter. She had lost interest in the circle and her elaborate system and did not seem to want to talk much. What little she said was about the hospital itself: she was trying to help the doctors, they didn't know how to treat the patients but they wouldn't listen to her. Most of those inside were getting worse rather than better; many had to stay there because no-one would take the responsibility of looking after them, even if they were drugged into manageability. They were poor, without relations; the hospital would not let them go away by themselves. She told him about one girl from farther north who thought she was a caribou.

She hardly glanced at the water-colour paints, though she thanked him sluggishly. Her eyes, normally wide and vivacious, were puffed shut nearly to slits and her skin appeared to have darkened. She reminded him of someone, though it took him several minutes to remember: it was an Indian woman he had seen early in the fall while he was still searching for a place to have a civilized drink. She had been sitting outside a cheap hotel with her legs apart, taking off her clothes and chanting, "Come on boys, what're you waiting for, come on boys, what're you waiting for." Around her a group of self-conscious, sniggering men had gathered. Morrison, against his will and appalled at her, the men and himself, had joined them. She was naked to the waist when the police got there.

When he rose to say goodbye Louise asked him, as if it was a matter of purely academic interest, whether he thought she would ever get out.

On his way out to the car it struck him that he loved her. The thought filled him like a goal, a destiny. He would rescue her somehow; he could pretend she was his cousin or sister; he would keep her hidden in the apartment with all his dangerous implements, razors, knives, nailfiles, locked away; he would feed her, give her the right drugs, comb her hair. At night she would be there in the sub-zero bedroom for him to sink into as into a swamp, warm and obliterating.

This picture at first elated, then horrified him. He saw that it was only the hopeless, mad Louise he wanted, the one devoid of any purpose or defence. A sane one, one that could judge him, he would never be able to handle. So this was his dream girl then, his ideal woman found at last: a disintegration, mind returning to its component shards of matter, a defeated form-less creature on which he could inflict himself like shovel on earth, axe on forest, use without being used, know without being known. Louise's notebook entry, written when she had surely been saner than she was now, had been right about him. Yet in self-defence he reasoned that his desire for her was not altogether evil: it was in part a desire to be reunited with his own body, which he felt less and less that he actually occupied.

Oppressed by himself and by the building, the prison he had

just left, he turned when he reached the main road away from the city instead of toward it: he would take his car for a run. He drove through the clenched landscape, recalling with pain the gentle drawl of the accommodating hills east and south, back in that settled land which was so far away it seemed not to exist. Here everything was tightlipped, ungiving, good for nothing and nothing.

He was halfway to the zoo before he knew he was going there. Louise had said it was kept open all winter.

Not much of the day was left when he reached the entrance: he would be driving back in darkness. He would have to make his visit short, he did not want to be caught inside when they locked the gates. He paid the admission fee to the scarved and muffled figure in the booth, then took his car along the empty drives, glancing out the side window at the herds of llama, of yak, the enclosure of the Siberian tiger in which only the places a tiger might hide were to be seen.

At the buffalo field he stopped the car and got out. The buffalo were feeding near the wire fence, but at his approach they lifted their heads and glared at him, then snorted and rocked away from him through the haunch-deep snowdunes.

He plodded along the fence, not caring that the wind was up and chilling him through his heavy coat, the blood retreating from his toes. Thin sinister fingers of blown snow were creeping over the road; on the way back he would have to watch for drifts. He imagined the snow rising up, sweeping down in great curves, in waves over the city, each house a tiny centre of man-made warmth, fending it off. By the grace of the power plant and the gas plant: a bomb, a catastrophe to each and the house would close like eyes. He thought of all the people he barely knew, how they would face it, chopping up their furniture for firewood until the cold overcame. How they were already facing it, the Koreans' fishes fluttering on the clothesline like defiant silver flags, the woman downstairs shrilling *Whispering Hope* off-key into the blizzard, Paul in the flimsy armour of his cheap nationalism, the landlady holding aloft torchlike her bar of soap stuck with artificial flowers. Poor Louise, he saw now what she had been trying desperately to do: the point of the circle, closed and self-sufficient, was not what it included but what it shut out. His own efforts to remain human, futile work and sterile love, what happened when it was all used up, what would he be left with? Black trees on a warm orange wall; and he had painted everything white....

Dizzy with cold, he leaned against the fence, forehead on mittened hand. He was at the wolf pen. He remembered it from his trip with Louise. They had stood there for some time waiting for the wolves to come over to them but they had kept to the far side. Three of them were near the fence now though, lying in its shelter. An old couple, a man and a woman in nearly identical grey coats, were standing near the wolves. He had not noticed them earlier, no cars had passed him, they must have walked from the parking lot. The eyes of the wolves were yellowish-grey: they looked out through the bars at him, alert, neutral.

"Are they timber wolves?" Morrison said to the old woman. Opening his mouth to speak, he was filled with a sudden chill rush of air.

The woman turned to him slowly: her face was a haze of wrinkles from which her eyes stared up at him, blue, glacial.

"You from around here?" she asked.

"No," Morrison said. Her head swung away; she continued to look through the fence at the wolves, nose to the wind, short white fur ruffled up on edge.

Morrison followed her fixed gaze: something was being told, something that had nothing to do with him, the thing you could learn only after the rest was finished with and discarded. His body was numb; he swayed. In the corner of his eye the old woman swelled, wavered, then seemed to disappear, and the land opened before him. It swept away to the north and he thought he could see the mountains, white-covered,

their crests glittering in the falling sun, then forest upon forest, after that the barren tundra and the blank solid rivers, and beyond, so far that the endless night had already descended, the frozen sea.

ISBN 0 88750 235 0 (hardcover)
ISBN 0 88750 236 9 (softcover)

Design by Michael Macklem

Printed in Canada

PUBLISHED IN CANADA BY OBERON PRESS